PSYCHOTIC
delusions

PSYCHOTIC

delusions

CJ MOORE

iUniverse, Inc.
Bloomington

Psychotic Delusions

iUniverse books may be ordered through booksellers or by contacting:

iUniverse
1663 Liberty Drive
Bloomington, IN 47403
www.iuniverse.com
1-800-Authors (1-800-288-4677)

Because of the dynamic nature of the Internet, any web addresses or links
contained in this book may have changed since publication and may no longer be
valid. The views expressed in this work are solely those of the author and do not
necessarily reflect the views of the publisher, and the publisher hereby disclaims
any responsibility for them.

Any people depicted in stock imagery provided by Thinkstock are models,
and such images are being used for illustrative purposes only.

Certain stock imagery © Thinkstock.

ISBN: 978-1-4697-0063-2 (sc)
ISBN: 978-1-4697-0064-9 (e)

Printed in the United States of America

iUniverse rev. date: 12/21/2011

Introduction

RALPH BARNS HAD it all, the perfect home and a nice job. The Barns were just your typical modern day middle class Afro-American family living in William Town, North Carolina. None of this was enough for Ralph. He had to go outside of his marriage. Now he may be paying for his foolish mistake by being stalk by a craze scorn lover. Not knowing the risk, he may have put his family in. What he thought was an undercover booty call on the side now has become a natural born killer in the small community.

Kim Jenkins was never good at dealing with rejection. Kim should have known better to put her trust in a marry man and since she was off of her medication for schizophrenic her killing spree had begun, her and her pet bird Larry.

Liz ever so faithful wife of Ralph thought that she had came from much more upper class than the people of William Town among her did. Little did she know it would take losing Ralph for the Lord not work it out but for her instead to take matters in her own hands.

It will be up to Sheriff Deidra Coates to solve the case of

a missing girl and a homicide caseall in one week. Like a young priest, giving his trial sermon this was Deidra Coates first case. With the help of newfound psychic, Maggie Stokes Sheriff Coates may even shine.

Mɪssʏ Bᴀʀɴs ʟᴏᴏᴋᴇᴅ outside through her window while her mother scolded her irritably, she had made her mother upset by staying out late over her friend's Egypt. Missy was the middle child of her sisters. Margret and Annabelle have always gotten along together with each other. Missy thought Margret was too fat and tall and she was way to bossy. Annabelle; on the other hand was excessively pretty for her own good. Being the youngest she thought that Annabelle was extremely spoil for her own good. Margret always thought both of them receive excessively much attention. Missy thought she was the most misunderstood. "Missy do you hear me talking to you?" her mom asked. Missy rolled her eyes and smacked her lips at what her mother said "Girl you are too hard headed for your own good." "Missy Bernice Barns!" shouted her mother. "If you don't get in here while I'm talking to you ...You better." Missy walked back to her room. Hesitantly she walked because she was tired of listening to her mother go on and on about nothing. It did not take that much to set her off Missy believed that her mother had an incredible ability of not understanding her at all. She thought trying to explain stuff to her mother was just like pulling teeth, a waste of time, a simple commodity she could not afford to waste. Liz could be reason with when you caught her in the right mood. Missy knew how to get on her side .She would cunningly change the subject or blurt out someone is secret that she was too keep. She would pull no punches nothing to her it seems was sacred. For some reason Liz, seem to always hounding her Missy thought. She thought that she was better than then the both of her sisters were. 'Missy the next time you go off and stay like you're crazy I am going to show you something!"Liz rambled. "Mom guessed what I've found out," Missy cleverly change the subject. "Egypt thinks she is pregnant!" shouted Missy. 'For real!" cried Liz. It was not true but the lie was efficient enough to quiet her mother down. "See I told you all about those fast behind tails girls." "Mom I know that you taught us better that. I love you too much to hurt you like Egypt done her folks," Missy said. What Missy thought about lying was as a dog thought about peeing outside. The news was almost too good to hold Liz thought although the idea of telling what she knew incubated to her. "Nope that just would not be the Christian thing to do," Liz thought to herself. She had always consider herself of a higher quality she did not like to mix with the common people were still Ralph, for some reason he wanted to mingle with the little folks. Liz did not know what to do with him. It was like a challenge to get him to act accordingly to society there was small people everywhere in this world. It would be up to her to decide where she wanted to look as a successful pillar in society or a hopeless wannabe and a loser in reality. It really did not matter what she did she always tried to do it better than anybody else did. Liz did not have that much growing up. She always had a plan to succeed in society, but she always kept in mind how much better off she was compare to most ordinary folks. She made good on the one promise she made to her mother never to marry down or below her level. She liked the fact that her husband Ralph was so easy and simple. He had met her one-day working at a convenience store nearby her house. ; It was the day he walk into her life. He looked so good to her when he walked in. She remembered how nervous she was but was still able to count his money without dropping it. After having a brief conversation with him, she realized that they had a lot in common. They both like nice things and did not mind working hard to get them. They promoted Ralph to chief mechanic where he worked. He had moved up in just five years and was extremely pleased with himself. Because most of his supervisors thought, he was the best. He loved when a situation came up at his job like a machine breaking down and no one able to repair it Ralph would gloat in his pompous idea of how good he were. However, he loved the fact how the plant could not run without him. Even when the plant slows down they would always find something for him to do. They would not send him home they would just let him ride the clock. Lord forbids the cost of production. Ralph made money for the plant the plant where he fined tranquility in his mind.

Ralph thought Liz Scratch was a fine woman who was built fully loaded from head to toe. He wondered why such a peach such as her had not been pluck. Therefore, Ralph and Liz eventually married and they had a nice little family. Ralph was especially proud of his girls; all of them even Missy. At times Ralph thought that Missy could be a little bit rambunctious. However, when it came to Annabelle his love for her was indubitable. Liz believes that Ralph spoiled her; one more thing Ralph ineffectually saw. Ralph also was very dear to his first-born Margret. Over the years, Margret metabolism began to slow down for her but she still love food. When it came to food, she became emotionally starve for it. Margret had even begun to develop a second chin. Ralph thought she would be a good homemaker. She would clean a whole house within a single day. Ralph wondered why no one come calling for his daughter. Was it the fact she was so shy? Ralph thought that Bob Wilson's son Myron would be the ideal catch for his daughter. Myron Wilson was every parents dream. He was a hard worker around the house and was smart in school. Just a responsible individual all the way round in a nut shell. Margret was becoming a grown beautiful young woman. Ralph truly felt like he had the best girls in the world. However, what Ralph did not know then was about to

4

debilitate his relationships with his girls. Margret was slowly coming out of her shell taking her own time to evolve and become beautiful and inquisitive. However, dating and in love with her friend Carlos Chavez you would think such news as this would make most people ecstatic .Not Ralph, Lord forbid the petal he had put his daughters upon. However, sometimes we all come short and fall down and it take a real man to admit that he drop the ball in life; shame on him if he does not get up do you agree? Ralph was looking at how perfect his daughters were. Margret, Missy and Annabelle were very endearing to his heart and soul.

Liz sat down on her old leather sofa contemplating on the news she heard today. She was thinking on how good she had it. So much better than most of her neighbors especially Egypt's parents she thought. Marring Ralph Barns was a good choice she had made. Twenty years ago Liz did not think that she be in this position. Liz Barns consider herself to be an enormous pillar in the stag net community of Williams Town. The small little people there just regular hard working, factory plant working honest people. It was not as if none of them had an excuse for their economics. Liz chuckled to herself about a recent incident that took place a couple weeks ago. Maggie Stokes; Liz next-door neighbor had come over to her house with a basket of rotting apples. You could smell the worms in front of her door. "Oh thank you Jesus Maggie how have you been doing?" Liz asked. Liz thought that there had to be better groups of Salvation Army donations that Maggie could have put on. "Oh I was just thinking about some of your fresh pies," said Liz. Yes, Maggie had been a hard worker. What did that get her? Nothing but years of hard work and misery thought Liz. These people were so content with their itty little lives it was pathetic. Even though her family did not have that much to offer society, still she felt she had the best chance of becoming important in her community. In most people lives, it did not take long for arrogance to define a person. In Liz case, it happens all at once. Now everything was going well in Ralph and Liz life until Ralph started to have an affair. That was the reason when the phone rang Ralph felt very edgy. The woman on the phone had the wrong number is wife told him. That was another narrow escape Ralph thought to him. He had met Kim at work on his job. His duty was to train her but he did not realize how close they had become. Ralph remembered when Kim brought him some of his favorite cook pigtails to eat at work. When Kim had a problem, he would all ways be that attentive ear she needed. Beside she was very easy to look at. "Ralph do you hear me?" Liz asked. "I swear the whole house could be burning down and you wouldn't still hear me!" Liz shouted. Yes he was becoming aware on how little attention he was paying to the woman he promise to who every word he would obey.

Missy eases back into her room her only place of totally solitude. The sound of the telephone rang broke the clean crisp silence of her room. "Hey girl is you going to the dance Friday night?" her friend Dense asked. Missy had forgotten all about the dance. She really did not know why that happens it was only the most happing thing going on in this little hick town. "God, Denise and Robert must be on the brink of another break up ", thought Missy .Because how would she find the time to go to a dance? "No girl these folks over here are tripping," Missy said. "Aim sorry to hear about that girl we all have our crosses to bear, I heard that it's going to be the bomb", said Denise. "Yeah girl, how about Robert tripping again "Missy tried to sound over the phone like she was surprise at what Denise was saying. "That nagger must be going crazy if he thinks that I'm keep telling him every day that I love him," said Denise. Missy laughs over on the phone. "I know that's right he better get out of here with that bull crap. The next thing he will want to ....well you know what I am talking about girl 'laugh Denise. Missy was really thinking about her little bow Bobby. She remembers how close it came from them doing it. Only strict discipline and level heads prevailed.

Ralph was wondering what if Kim was trying to get in contact with him; he had started something that he had to finish now. What had begun as a lustful and sweet sin now has become something that was endangering and strange. This love affair would be something that Kim would be starving for now on. Even though something that started out sweet and innocent somehow now has become evil. Ralph was ready for this to end, and it had to end. Liz was a good loving woman at times, but he just could not keep putting up with her arrogance when it came to most of the people he knew. However, that just only aggravated him. Ralph thought getting rid of Kim is going to be hell. She was a tiny little woman half afro-American and Cherokee with a big butt and a condense tempera woman who would wear a different color wig at times accordingly what mood she was in. However, how fine she would be if only she could keep her mouth shut and acted with a little reprieve, he thought. Tomorrow is where he would end this.

Annabelle Barns was always singing to herself when she cleaned her room; it made her feel good when she sang. She did not like a lot of clutter unlike her older sister Missy. "I believe you got some kind of nervures disorder?" asked Missy. That was all Missy knew how to do and that was putting people down, thought Annabelle. "You're just jealous no one came to clean your little clutter box," marked Annabelle. "Yeah whatever you say butt wipe, "Missy replied. This type of dialogue would go on all day on a typical day. This oration of wits would only cease when the phone or Momma Liz in intervene. Sometimes Margret would just look at them being the oldest she tried to be a prime example. Margret would get the advantage over her sibling always beating them to the punch and by out telling on them. However, what Margret was to find out about her whole wide world would be a good example of realism gone wrong. It is funny sometimes when you think your persona does not stink along comes an individual to point out your imperfections by a dilapidated life like Melvin Little.

Maggie Stokes was tired from standing in line for her housing voucher. She had arrived there early that morning and assumes she would be the first to get taking care of. God, tomorrow Food Stamps Day another long tiring event, she thought to herself. It had been hard for her every since Sal, her husband passed away. He was a good man but had a drinking problem and was a well-known womanizer. Maggie thought the liquor would be his demise. Instead, a freak accident claims his life. Sal was an angler by trade and in a bizarre incident; he fell over board and drowned. Having two widows at the funeral, his lawful wife and his common law one only explicated the rumors Maggie heard about. Pooches Evans; the other woman in Sal life. She had some nerve showing up at the funeral service. The two-woman relationship was to say in the least intolerable but over threw the years they seem to manage. However there was one little episode where Sal carelessness cause her a visit to the health department. She had never felt so embarrass being there. She was able to get through that and among other things in her life. Dealing with this world alone can be challenge and tired. Maggie kept on proceeding because she had a strong belief that only the Lord had something better for her in her life.

ᴇARLY Mᴏɴᴅᴀʏ ᴍᴏʀɴɪɴɢ Ralph decided to end his love affair with Kim. The more he thought about his marriage the more he realizes he needed it and wanted it. He demonstrated that fact last night to Liz. He thought he would pick up a fast breakfast from McDonald this morning since Liz was sound asleep.

Kim Jenkins also was awake and ready to go to work it was a routine event in the Jenkins house getting Melvin kids ready was a handful especially when there was no help from her live in boy friend Melvin. Early that year Melvin did help get her off the streets and now the only man that she wanted to touch her was Ralph Barns. He truly loved her as if a real man could not like her sorry behind ex-husband Melvin. How could she have been involved with him in the first place "she wondered? Melvin was good at playing ball in high school but now he was only good for three things ,making babies, coming up with schemes and pipe dreams and oh yeah finding good excuses for not going to work. She had lost feelings for him a long time ago and it was easy for Ralph to come into her life. He put a brand new spark into her life and she was like a piece of dried out kindle wood she was ready to become a flame.

At 2:30 pm, that afternoon was the time Margret had planned to meet Carlos at his job. She would often meet him there on payday and from there they would do lunch or some other festivities they enjoy. Today was not payday of all the others time they met this day was different. With tears in her eyes, she knew that eventually she would have to get rid of this freight of guilt. It was only just a careless fluke one too many drinks at the bar that night" she tried to tell herself. However, whatever a rationalization she try to rationalize did not help any. Now I got to tell this good man that my baby may not be his," Margret thought then another tear gently roll down her cheek. Margret was in and out of deep thought and concentration. How could she let one little slip up ruined her life

Annabelle was in her room watching her favorite show. While in great consumption of the T.V news of the Celebrity All Star, she heard her cell phone receiving a text. The message was from her fried Pam explaining how happy she was because her dad had promise her that if she got out and land a job he would help her buy a car. That was last year but today she was hire at the Just Us Chicken Shack. Annabelle said to "herself um some girls have all the luck." A big nice red Hummer with some nice rims now that is what I am talking about Annabelle thought to herself. However, she did not want to spend the rest of her summer in side of a grease can all of her summer. There she was thinking again grabbing the cart before the horse. She had not gotten her license it and she knew that her dad would have a fit if he knew that she was even thinking about getting her license she never forgot how he acted when she decided to take off her training wheels off her bike when she was nine years old. She knew her limitation when came to stuff like that. Pam was her best friend but she could be beside herself at times. It was no way around it she would have to get her parents to sign up for her to try for driving license any way. Unless someone else could step up to the plate and do it for her. They would not know anything until it was too late Annabelle thought. She wondered if Pam would help her out.

Carlos Chavez was cleaning down his machine he was taking his time wiping off his machine because he thrives in perfection. He also had a house he wanted to show her. Margret always seems to be wise when it came to money and he trusts her judgment. Carlos also had good news for Margret, his future wife to be. He just only had to find a way to ask her hand in marriage. Therefore, he decided to give her the very best news first. Barany Tubs, Carlos boss seem as if he was interested in giving him a promotion and he knew how much Margret would love to hear that. That was the reason he was running late, Carlos took his time today so he could give his machine a good cleaning. He had only been working there for less than six months and already he was faster than most of the people out there. Carlos tried to look proficient by his machine as he wipes the apparatus he saw Mr. Hobbs on his way to speak to him."Son I sure like the way you clean that baby "said Mr. Hobbs. 'Thank you sir" 'Carlos said nervously he tried to treat every interaction with Mr. Hobbs as if he was doing his last interview; at moments like this he tried to be careful. Barany Hobbs loved going over schematics with his employees especially the ones he plans to promote. He likes to see young enthusiastic employees like Carlos working in his plant. "Carlos I have good news to tell you. We are experiencing a reduction in our dye department production and we want you to help head in management as assistant manager," Mr. Hobbs said. "Sir thanks you for this opportunity and I promise you that you will not regret this," said Carlos. "Well of course you know this job comes with a huge paid raise," Mr. Hobbs said. "Of course," said Carlos. Now it seems to Carlos that for the first time in his life everything was coming together. He had the right boss and job and he had the right women. Now all he needed was just what every red blooded American wanted a nice home and family.

L IZ WOKE UP this morning with exuberating energy she wondered why, being that she was up all night with her man. "God that man still know how to love me "she said out loud to herself as she bounces around the kitchen singing cleaning her tables. She had slept in late that morning because she would usually be up before nine in the morning. She walked down the hallway from where the girl's room was. She was impressed how neat their beds appear. It seem like everybody wanted to be neat today even Missy. While Liz was doing her morning inspection, she heard her doorbell rang she wonder who it was this early this morning. It was one of her card-playing friends Goldie, whom she converse with on bridge night. She would keep her up to date on the news. . She was a three-time divorcee in her fifties, a dark skin afro American who thought she had a banging figure for her age. "How you doing this morning girl" asked Goldie as she reach into her purse pulling out a cigarette trying to pacify her two pack a day nicotine habit. "Girl let me tell you about your girl Ann," Goldie excitedly ranted. Ann was another one of Liz bridge friends she met on Wednesday night. "She got it all she got the hold damn house," Goldie cried. "Tell me what happen girl" asked Liz in earnest. Goldie was very informative known for giving the 411 down on every situation she met; yes, she was a very noise woman. "Ann caught John red handed with his draws down his ankles in their kitchen with the babysitter. Girl all I know is I heard the judge say guilty and house!" Goldie said high fiving Liz almost falling down onto the sofa. That what that increment get find not even having the decencies to get a room 'Liz thought but she felt bad for Ann. They had got married almost the same time or about the same time as her and Ralph. That was what she like most of her husband; his dependability to be there for her it was him Liz places her whole heart in and where the most she would never have to go down that road of devastation.

Ralph arrives early at Shack ford Industry, a company that one of his high school friends started. Brad Shack ford was an energetic businessperson whom Cash Money magazine held as one of the most successfully business of the year for the town of Williams Town North Carolina. He and Brad had not been that close growing up in school. I guess you could say the two individuals from a different cloth. Brad Shack ford came from a rich family of wealth who still believe in making money the old fashion way. Both of them believe in diligent work would paid off in the end. Ralph like his down time of average of production; the time a machine that was down not running, because of repairing the machine would speed up production and make more money. Ralph was a valuable man for the plant in this way. "Raphine boy its looks like it will be another grand year" his boss said joyfully. Ralph hated when he calls him that and especially when he patted his head as if he was a little kid or something. "I am concern about those new Ker matrices machine you all just ship in from China, yes this year do look promising "said Ralph. "Yeah that's what I like about you the most Ralph you know how to keep those ragged bastards running and making us money." 'Yeah I bet you do, Ralph thought himself. Brad ramble on and on about the news of the company Ralph was listen although in the back of his mind was what he going to do about his situation with Kim. Ralph kept telling himself to stay focus and keeping his eyes on the prize of comfort ability; that is his home and his wife. Kim was to him was like a forbidden liaison that he tasted and now it was time to let that flavor go. It was ten minutes before brake.

Soon it would be time for Ralph to meet Kim, something they had done over through the years a meeting of their minds and their deep concerns.

MAGGIE STOKES WAS up early that morning bending down in the middle of her collard green row. Bending down these days has become a chore for Margret how in the world did she ever find the energy she wonders. One minute it would be arthritis or gout the next it would be aching bones and still she thought she had it better than most people she knew. She had a chance almost on a daily basis to meet them. At Greater Comfort Home for disable and blind people she was constantly reminded of how bless she was. A member of her church invited her to minister out there. However, Maggie did not know how therapeutic it would be for her. There was a point in her life where she did not feel like even going on. There was a time when she did not feel anything when Sal died. No, man no Angel or God for that matter could feel that void. Not saying Sal was all that but he was all the man she knew. That was a very bad time in her life and she was able to get threw it 'the Lord will not put no more on you than you can bear' she thought. Now she has found great meaning in her life by giving her help to others especially the patients at Great Comfort Home. It was a good feeling to her and in some way to be love.

MARGRET WAITED INSIDE the lobby of the plant of Shack Ford industry waiting patiently and in earnest wondering what the next moments was going to bring. Now that she had, time to think about it girl's night out had been quiet silly and ridiculous Margret would never forgive her. She could hear the intercom announcing that Carlos had a visitor in the lobby waiting for him. She only had a moment to tell him everything. Early that day she had visited her doctor who had administered the test in which delivered her the bad news. Of all the people that had gotten her pregnant why did, it had to be Melvin Jenkins, some person she hardly even knew. He had told her over a few drinks how he and his old woman was not getting along. The idea to sleep with him must have come from Westside of Hell. It seem like the Tavares Gin told her to go on with her bad self. "If he really truly cares about you then he will understand. It will not matter that you went out with a totally stranger and let him relieve himself inside of you. Na it won't even matter," the more she thought about the idea inside of her head it was like beating a dead horse in to making some sense in her mind. To believe that it did not matter Margret was not foolish enough to risk her life gambling whether Carlos would one day find it in his heart to forgive her. He was a hell of a man but every man had his limits and she did not wanted to test the boundaries. It was a wonder to her how he talk about loving her and taking good care of her and marring her and building a house and a family together. The ugly truth would have to take its place in silence. The horn in the lobby sounded loud threw out the entire plant. Almost nerve racking if you were not use to it. In walk Carlos with his heart pounding about to explode with the good news of his promotion. He could hardly wait to hold her and tell her the good news.

Ralph walk into his office to go over the schematics figures with Brad when his telephone rang. "Hello baby I forgot to tell you to have a bless day and I love you," said Liz. "Thank you sweet heart I'll talk to you later honey let me go over these figures with Brad" Ralph told Liz. It seem like their love for each other was getting stronger these days. "Now Ralph ire you telling me the projectiles for this fall are mark up?" Brad asked. 'Yes and that is the reason we should jump on this lot fast before the Johnston plant recognize its vulnerability "answered Ralph. He seems to be making some headway with Brad about Lot C when there was a knock on his door. In walk the most pretty pair blue jeans, baby brown eyes Ralph had ever seen. "Damn "Ralph said as he shook his head Kim Jenkins was a fine piece of woman to him. What they were talking about seemed to interest Kim. "I brought you some coffee, excuse me if I interrupted that sound interesting," said Kim. 'Well Barns I'll be getting back with you on the figures" said Brad as he left abruptly because of Kim's presence. 'Well well" does your husband know what you are wearing to work at times?" Ralph asked pretending to be mad but really turn on .Stay focus remembers the prize," he kept telling himself. 'Ms .Jenkins we will have to have a meeting just you and me I thank we need to have a talk about your performance. I think it's pathetic." Kim look around in the room as if there was someone else in the office beside her "What do you mean Ms

Jenkins. Whatever happens to Kim baby? Whatever happens to it feels so good Kim baby Hun Ralph.?" Kim had a bad way in dealing with rejection and she could smell it a mile away. With Ralph, she thought that things were to get better for her. 'Calm down please Kim I love you but I am not in love with you, baby I want the best for you but I am not the best for you. My heart belongs to someone else!" shouted Ralph.

KIM FELT RIGHT then as if someone pull the rug right from under her heart. How could he of all people do her like that as if she was just some distance whore sat along the highway and discarded? "Listen Negro no um it's not going to go down like this. No un Claude!" shouted Kim. Times when Kim gets mad, she would blurt out fragment and bits lines of her favorite movies. 'Woman you knew what this was. I told you in the beginning not to fall in love with me. I love you but damn it I not in love with you" said Ralph. "Do you know how many nights that I went to bed without letting Melvin touch me?" ranted Kim. "Yeah yeah and I am still not leaving my wife okay!" shouted Ralph. "Do you get it now?" he asked "Yes Ralph I get it finally I see the problem" said Kim. She then turned around and clapped her hands in the air as if she was killing an imaginary pest; he had seen her blow up before. Never had he witness her go from hysterical to cool calm and collective. 'Yes Ralph I see what the problem is. It's that bitch name Liz is written all over it " said Kim .That was all Ralph heard from her beside the loud bang from his office door and the click clack sound of her high heels going down the hall way. "Kim! Kim! Kim!" Ralph shouted. He knew she heard him yelling after her. Ralph went back into his office to navigate his next move. Should he call Kim later on to do damage control or go home to Liz and lay the loving on thick. The choice seem very clear to him. Home to Ralph was where he found compatible stability conscience and comfortably in his marriage to Liz. Somehow, for one second he took his eyes off the prize and the prize meaning his marriage. He also wonder what kind of mental exam did the company had to offer their employees because he was beginning to believe Kim, that bitch was crazy.

A NNABELLE WAS IN her bedroom going over the signs test for her driver's license. Such icons she barely notices while riding. However, this time she was determine to get her ounce of freedom. She knew if she did her part daddy would do his. Even though it was not that candy apple, red jeep Hummer that she craved it would be a set of wheels that Annabelle needed. Deep down Annabelle knew that anything she wanted she could have. Her father's love was unadulterated she knew that she had always been his favorite daughters found great comfort in that fact alone But that was the reason why she did not let Fredrick go all the way last year at the prom. The last thing she wanted to do was bring the Barnes name in shame. The song on her cell phone rang aloud "Give Love on Christmas Day" by Michael Jackson was the ring tone Annabelle chose. She let the song play on and on because she did not feel like talking to Fredrick who was on the line. It seems like these days there was only one thing on his mind these days and Annabelle did not feel like arguing. Her cell phone kept going off until Annabelle got tired of the sound of the song and turn her phone off. Then in came Liz ranting about the disturbance that Fredrick was causing."Belle what is wrong with you and why want you answer the phone? That boy been calling here like that all day!" said Liz. She did not like her home to be disrespect like that. Annabelle knew that her mother would not put up with her boy friend antics for long. "Mom I don't know what is the matter with Fredrick. It's like I not paying him enough attention or something," said Annabelle. However, Annabelle knew the real reason why

Fredrick was acting as he was about to go out of his mind. She knew that her mother would not understand the reason why Fredrick was acting like a fool. It seems what her mom had failed to realize was her youngest little girl was growing into a beautiful young woman. Annabelle knew what she had promise the boy.

Sometimes Liz had a hard time understanding her children 'one minute you think you know them the next you realize you barely knew them at all. "It's not good for that boy to be running around here like he has lost his damn mind, are you sure you all have not done anything?"Liz asked. No of course not" answer Annabelle the only thing that she and Fredrick had done was kiss, maybe a little seductively but safe sexually. Her cell phone was sounding off again but this time it was her friend Karen Annabelle answers it in a sign of relief. Karen was at home trying to build up the nerves to forge the signature of Annabelle's father permission slip. It was a big deal if she were caught not only she be expel but also Karen. 'What going on girl?" asked Annabelle? Annabelle knew that Karen had come through. Annabelle knew that she was misbehaving badly by not waiting for her father to sign the permission forms but she did not feel like going through the drama of hope and let down, "Well Ann you should not have any problems Wednesday providing you have the insurance information" Karen told her. It would be worth it Annabelle kept telling herself maybe now she would have time for Fredrick. "I hope this little caper here will work and Lord knows I sure don't need to be caught" Annabelle said. 'I feel you Miss goodie two shoes," Egypt answered. Wednesday morning she would have to meet Mr. Cox the driver's Ed instructor. She knew that he had a wide range of questions being the fact that he knew her dad very well.

KIM NEEDED HER pills she often took to calm her down. For some reason she could not remember where she had put them. She had started back seeing and hearing things again all of this because lack of her medication. Her guardian angel, pet parrot had been coming to her again. Kim had thought that part of her life was over. She has not seen Larry in years. He only came to her when she was in trouble or something she had done wrong. It seem like the only thing that Larry knew was about evil things. When he first started talking to her, he had only good advice to for her. He blames her for letting his cage open and for her cat eating him. He never forgave her for her negligence and he decided to ruin her life liked she ruin his. "Shut up Larry I am not even paying you any mind," Kim shouted at her invisible friend. She could not believe such evil could come in a form as Larry. He had a nasty habit of profanity and smoking. Her brightly color friend had a glass spectacle on his left eye. He was colored blue up top and green and yellow in the mid section and had orange feet and yellow toes. Kim was amaze to see how he could smoke; being that the cigar was about one fourth of his head and he could talk, Not only that he could cuss you .out. "I don't know who you looking at bitch you are straight up tripping." cussed Larry. Over these years she had gotten use to Larry vulgarizes since it was her fault of his demise. She looked at Larry as he spanned around to show her that he had her pill bottle. "Looking for this bitch?"Larry asked with a grin. 'Leave me alone just leave me Larry!" Kim shouted.

KIM JENKINS WAS looking on the internet to find her next location where she would make her move. She had put all of her faith in Ralph the very one thing she had promise herself not to do. She just wanted to leave town and start all over. All that she was to Ralph was a piece of tail and now she knew that. Even though she had not met Liz, it did not stop her from having a deep-seated hatred for her. Now she knew how Ralph. Really felt and where his heart was .Now she realizes the key of hurting Ralph was hurting where his heart was at and that was with Liz. The very thought intoxicated her intellect but reasoning said no Kim."Stab stabbed the bitch," said Larry. Seldom do rational people like her usually think rational after being hurt. In addition, she was tired of being rational now she was out of medication and ready to hurt. She really did not have that much against Liz other than how she disliked the fact that Ralph still loved her and that fact alone cause her to hate the bitch. However, what was she to do for money. She definitely could not quit her job now; an idea she had entertain, and she could not depend on Melvin since he was practically out of her life. As she walks back and forth from her bedroom to her living room, she contemplated how she could win Ralph back from Liz. She had hoped it would not come to this. She was just tired of moving and starting all over again. The more she thought about it the madder she got.

"Hey how about we forget everything that happens today. Okay?" Ralph asked. "Thank you Ralph I know how to play my position from now on. I just still care about you. I guess I will always", said Kim in anguish. Ralph heard his wife approaching the den and he hurried up with his call. "Hey I got to go I will see you tomorrow", said Ralph. "Yeah I guess I will", said Kim. She just sat in her bedroom looking at her floor. There was great emptiness in side of her heart. She was going over in her mind all of the promises Ralph had made. Only the sounds of Melvin snoring broke the silence in her house. "Kill that bitch and his whole entire clan all must die," said Larry. Kim fantasy fowl just stood there with his wicked evil grin ready to give his evil instructions to Kim. She felt compel to listen to him. Kim realizes that it was time to score some medication. Larry, who was once just a voice inside of her head, was slowly coming alive and very real. Kim reaches into the cabinet in the kitchen for some Tylenol. She would often take the medicine for her throbbing headache she often got when her mind played chess matches with Larry. Now it seemed like Larry wicked instructions had started to prevail Kim's cognitive thinking.

ARGRET SAT QUIET in preparing herself on what she had planned to tell Carlos. She looked around at the other young women in the lobby who any of them could have their eyes on her man."Hey darling you are looking at Shack Ford newest lead personal "Carlos said. She h ad not notice him standing there in front of her with his full apparel on. Carlos had his wet suit on and his green hat on which emphasize leadership on his floor. Margret could see by the smile on his face how proud he was. "Baby you got it!" Margret shouted. She than grab him and kiss him with merriment and hug him. "Yeah baby girl I did it without the old man help I got the promotion," said Carlos. He was glad that he did not do what Margret had asked him to do and that was to ask her father for the promotion. Margret was happy that her man was able to find his way in the world without the help of her influences. Carlos was a proud man in deed. His family came from the Dominican Republic. His family first arrives in the United States in the mid eighties. Carlos family knew all about struggle. It was a lesson they learn from day one. Margret had a second thought come in her mind. She just could not live with a lie of that malamute. Conscience would not let her rest. The hand on the lobby's breakroom clock said 6:00pmwhich meant Carlos would soon be off. It was time to find out how much Carlos really lov her.

MAGGIE STOKES LOOKED at around in her room. As if waiting for some divine answer from Heaven way. She asks God to guide all of her decisions something lay in her bed well rested from the d before. It seem like she was always preparing to go to work. She look at the small alarm clock that sat on her dresser was preparing to sound off. That is what the time peace usually did. A little token she had gotten from her philandering husband Sal. A sound of emptiness fill the entire house as Maggie mind go back to the days when she was fill with joy. Sal would bring home objects that he found on his journeys away from home. Along with scavenger items, he would also do yards for other people in the neighborhood. Even though Sal drinks heavily, he seems to be in great shape. Maggie misses him very much it seem like he left her suddenly. The doctors' report was that he had drowned over board. Everyone at her church seems to Miss Sal. When it came to yard work, he did pretty work. Sal kept the Church graveyard in order and intact. Although' Sal had a roving eye for the women, deep down inside hereally love Maggie. Most of the time, Sal was a joy to be with. Sometimes pleasurable even, but when he drink a low grade of alcohol he could be downright mischievous sprite. At times, his favorite alcohol was Richards wine. Some Sundays Maggie managed to get him in the church. Sal would go on Sundays just to satisfy his wife. Most of the time when he did attend the services, his mind wonder and loose focus of the message and inside of him he had a personal battle of fighting sleep and a thirst for a cold one. On that faithful day when Sal fell overboard, Maggie instantly told Sal to be careful and not to be drinking. As usually, Sal got his drink on and fell into the pages of Bishop Clark eulogy program. Bishop Clark spoke of a good man who went to church on Sunday. He spoke of aman who paid his tithes es by keeping the Church lawn cut and trim. He spoke of a man who was a great family man and a good husband. However, the more that Bishop Clark spoked, the more Maggie glanced at the program to see if she was at the right funeral.

"Maggie he was a good man, Fred had his faults but tell me who don't", said Bishop Clark. On the day of Sal funeral, her church showed Maggie their appreciation. Not only Sal was the best yardman they had he was very reasonable when it came to his salary. Mother Bethel Moore narrated his eulogy."Gone too soon but he is with the Lord". That was her text in Sal eulogy. Now the days seem longer and harder without Sal being in her life.

L IZ MADE HERSELF busy all day cooking and cleaning she had attended her usually morning activities that day.

Liz Seiners' meetings she met on Thursday along with her best friend Goldie were very important to her. Goldie could always keep her laughing at something or another. Today topic was about food stamps and who receive them. "Yeah girl they saw her standing in the line; trying not to be seen" said Goldie. "Really?" asked Liz. She did not know that her neighbor Maggie Stokes was having hard times. "But she seem like she was always in a good spirits whenever I met her. Doesn't the church she belong to help her since she work so diligent there" asked Liz. "That's a good question you know how those people there are", said Goldie. The people at Moring Glory Freewill Baptist Church, under the leadership of Bishop Jake Clark carry out many social programs for the poor. Why did they not help Maggie?

A NNABELLE WOKE UP this morning with a minor sore throat and a slight fever. So she gargle her mouth out with salt water."Um I must be coming down with a cold", she said to herself. Annabelle heard the doorbell rang and ran down stairs shouting. "Mama Mama I got it", shouted Annabelle. She thought perhaps that it could be her friend Fredrick. Liz was up in the kitchen cooking breakfast as usually. Often she would become offended if you mess over your meal. When Annabelle answers the door, it was Liz friend Goldie. "Hey child how are you doing?" asked Goldie. "Oh fine maim .Are you doing alright Ms. Goldie "asked Annabelle. "Now what did I tell you about that. You make me feel so old "Goldie said. Liz came out of the kitchen to see her friend. She wondered what she would have to laugh about today. You could never tell with Goldie. She would have you hysterical at anything that came out of her mouth. "Hey Liz how have you been doing?' asked Goldie. 'Oh, fine just fine. I can't complain," said Liz. In the background of their conversation, you could hear Annabelle coughing her head off. 'Damn sound like Bronchitis' said Goldie. 'Honey is you alright. Baby girl perhaps you should take some days out from school!' shouted Liz. "Mom I am fine. I will be all right. It is not anything but the weather changing. The phone upstairs was ringing and Annabelle ran to answers it. For some reason Fredrick felt as if he was losing Annabelle to someone else but did not know who it was but something did not feel right with him. "What's have been you been doing?" Annabelle asked Fredrick. She knew how he was performing yesterday. She just did not time for his antics. "Look why did you act the fool on my mama phone yesterday. Hanging up and calling as if you are crazy! Keep it up and I swear to God Fredrick I'll leave you!" shouted Annabelle. "Belle you got me crazy. Why are you not talking to me?" asked Fredrick. Annabelle could hear the hurt in Fredrick voice through the phone. "Belle is there someone else?" asked Fredrick. "Where Fredrick tells me is that someone underneath you um?" asked Annabelle. This was not the time to be having this conversation with

Fredrick. She told him she would talk to him later because she really did not feel that well.

Ralph Barns was sound asleep this morning until he heard Goldie loud mouth. He heard her laughing aloud about something. 'I wonder what that strumpet lying about now?" wondered Ralph. He knew that Goldie had a reputation for carrying around news from house to house. "She needs to take care of her of her own damn house", Ralph muttered to himself. Ralph knew Goldie way back in high school. Even back then, she had a mouth on her. Now that he thought about it, Goldie did make Liz stand bout. Standing beside Goldie Liz stood out like a sore thumb. Liz swears to have been Goldie best friend.

Ralph was fortunate to run into Liz at the store that warm afternoon day in William Town. He was thankful for the years they share together. Deep in his heart, he realizes that Liz would be the only one for him. Ralph would no t accept anyone else in his life. Nevertheless, why did he fall so fast and deep for Kim? At first, everything began innocent. First was the innocent ride to work and then the innocent kiss with the ride to home. He had listened to Kim's problems and caught a feeling in the process. "What a good damn friend gone to waste" Ralph thought. However, he knew that in order for them to exist his marriage would have to end.

Annabelle went to the bathroom because she was feeling nauseous. The conversation with Fredrick did not help any. Liz stuck her head in the bathroom doorway. This was very unlike Annabelle to be feeling bad like she was. "Belle baby what is going on with you?" asked Liz. "Mom I must caught something in church Sunday. You know how it is when you are around a lot of people," said Annabelle. Liz had something to tell Annabelle. It was something Goldie had said. "Goldie believes that the flu has started in Williams Town. She even knew two others who call out sick from work," said Liz. "Mom I think what I need is some rest, that's it," said Annabelle. "Okay Belle, just be careful when you go outside," said Liz.

This was not normal for Annabelle to act the way she did over the phone. Maybe she got somebody else," thought Fredrick. Now he was finding himself listing to slow music. Usually a done somebody wrong song was what he found comfort. There were others girls he had in mind. It was only Annabelle Fredrick thought he had a future with. Even though he was eighteen years old and dead broke.

FREDRICK HEAD DROP when Annabelle scolded him. He realizes that he did not have any proof of any wrongdoing on her part. "Every time that I want to see you it is always an excuse for you not showing up" said Fredrick. "Look Fredrick I love you but you're too damn controlling", said Annabelle. Fredrick knew that he could had sat there all day and not got his point across to Annabelle. So he decided not to. "Hey what do you have plan for the rest of today. "I do not know Fredrick I do not feel too good right now. Maybe I might be feeling better later on," said Annabelle. Feeling like this was unusual for Annabelle. She rarely caught colds. It was very rare for her to feel strange or sluggish. She knew all that Fredrick really cares about was what his friends were getting and what he was not. This was the reason why she stayed away from him this long.

Annabelle hated drama and did not like to argue. Beside, the way she was feeling, she could care less how Fredrik felt. Ralph loved to sleep in late on Saturdays. It was his day off unless the plant calls him in on an emergency. He only hopes that he had made himself clear with Kim and he did not get any surprises.

Maggie was up early this morning. She had promise Bishop Oates she would coordinate Sunday dinner this week. Maggie was to be receiving help from her friend and lifetime member Ella Brooks. Ella had a recipe for the moist brownies. She was also a good organizer. "Now Margate you're cooking the collards. I just rode by your garden the other day. They look beautiful", said Ella. "Thanks, the name is Mrs. Maggie Stokes, I'll try but the Lord's willing," said Maggie. "Yes he is and with your collards greens and my secret recipe we can't lose, "said Ella. Both of the women wanted the recognition of their cooking skills. The moist bake brownies were Ella's signature. Many people thought maybe that she should market her recipe sensation. On the other hand, there were Maggie's collards greens, the best sweetest tender greens near East. Maggie had a way of season her greens with Splendor that gave her collards their unique taste. Even though there was not any physical contest, you would not have known it by looking at them.

Kim looks at her phone all day waiting to hear from Ralph. Deep down in her heart she knew she was waging a losing battle of holding on Ralph love. Now she realizes it was pain contrition. Perhaps, IT was the reason she had make up sex with Melvin or if you wanted to call it gets even sex. She wanted to call Ralph but she was damn well tired of apologizing for what she felt. She glances out of the corner of her eye at Melvin. "Oh God how I despise his ass," she said frowning at Melvin. Kim had only one weakness when it came to Melvin. In the bedroom, he could hold his own. It sure would be nice if he could do it also in the real world. "Eric, Deuce you boys get up for breakfast," Kim shouted. "Deana get up and use the bathroom," Kim shouted at Melvin's 4-year-old daughter. Now hearing Kim yelling at his 4year old did not fare too well with Melvin. Deana was his favorite and Duce the apples of his eye both of them from his first marriage. 'Come here baby girl, I know you're sleepy," said Melvin. "You see now that's what's wrong with her. You're spoiling her," said Kim.

Missy walked around the remainder of the day spraying her mouth with antiseptic. She was preparing herself for the worst. Annabelle stood in her door way and shock her head at Missy. "That's really unnecessary," said Annabelle. "Look you woke me up this morning with your coughing," said Missy. "I heard Goldie this morning saying something is going around Williams Town and I am not taking any chances," said Missy. Annabelle just stood there and shocked her head. At first Missy started to irritate Annabelle but then she thought a girl could not be too careful. Germs never been a problem with Annabelle but it seem like today it would be. For the first time in her young adult life, she would go to bed with a sore throat.

MAGGIE WAS ABOUT to get her bed ready for bedtime. She heard the phone ringing. Maggie wondered who could be calling her this time of the night."Sister stokes how you are doing?" asked Bishop Jack Clark. He had taken up an interest in her after Sal death. "Fine bishop I can't complain just a little headache that's all Bishop," said Maggie. "Now what did I tell you about that. It's Jack," said Bishop Jack Clark. No matter how good a friend the Bishop had been, she still did not feel comfort calling him Jack."Tell me how is the misses," said Maggie. "Oh she is fine. She wants to know if you be available next fourth Sunday?" asked Bishop Jack Clark. "Of course I am honor," said Maggie. She thought that the Bishop was getting to be a little too friendly. By asking her to be informal, she thought that was fresh. Now she had heard about his luncheons with her adversary Ella. She would do anything to become Bishop Jack Clark favorite member Maggie thought. Beside she had grown up with Edith, Bishop Clark wife. They were not friends but only acquaintance on an irregular basic. They got together only on church anniversaries and church ceremonies and luncheons. One of the reasons why Maggie did not care too much for Edith was because she thought she was better than everybody else was. Maggie did not like Edith. However, she would not that much as to sleep with her husband. She got up and stood at her full-length mirror. As she looked at herself in the mirror she admire how the years been good to her. At one time in her life, she was the homecoming queen of 1966 at John C Smith High School in Washington, North Carolina. Maggie took her religion seriously. She did the same when it came to her marriage vows. Sal has been dead for over ten years. Jack did not have a chance in hell to be with her.

Sunday morning came too soon for Margret. , she was to meet Maria Chavez the mother of Carlos. Margret felt like she was already on trail just before meeting Mrs. Chavez. She had a hard time trying not to be nervous."I wonder what kind of question she'll ask me," Margret asked herself. How long have you known my son? How many children do you want? And what kind of religion do you believe in?" Margret thought. The top three questions she thought would be ask by his mother yeah, and the most asked question of all, can you cook, the most important question of all. Margret knew that Carlos like a little starch in his food. Her specialty was Italian meatballs in noodles and cheese. Margret felt Carlos deserve a special dinner tonight to show his mother she indeed knew how to cook. Margret called Carlos too sees if he had got up yet. Today was First Sunday a day where most people visit other churches. One of the reasons Carlos slept in the day late was because he had work late Saturday night. Margret wanted to touch basic with Carlos for more information on tonight's topic. This would be the first time her family and Carlos sat down and had dinner together. Margret wanted everything to be just right. As she was cleaning her room, she heard Annabelle coughing her head consistently. Margret stopped in shock in her doorway to see her sister Annabelle out on her bedroom floor unconscious.

Liz heard Margret screaming that something wrong with Annabelle. She dropped everything she had in her hands and ran up the stairs. When she arrives to the top of the stairs, she saw Margret crying uncontrollably. Liz fell down to her knees and tried to wake Annabelle. "Margret call 911 hurry," shouted Liz. Margret ran and jump down two flight of stairs. All in the neighborhood of Williams Town that morning, you could hear the echoes of sirens going to the Barns house.

Dr. Patricia Bell was running around the hospital this morning like an inexperienced attendant. All this week she had an unusually amount of flue related symptoms from people. In addition, giving the fact this was not the time of the year for it. The rooms at Belfort Memorial were filling up with sick people that was coughing and throwing up. "Dirtball what are we going to do, the rooms are filling up?" asked Christina Ross, the new interim. Patricia was concern but she decided not to show it. 'If the situation worsens will get help from Clay Bottom Memorial," Dr. Bell said. A call came in on the intercom informing them to get a bed ready for Annabelle Barns. "Not Ralph baby girl," she thought. He and Patricia were friends in high school. Ralph was probably the person she should have married. "Dr. Bell we are running out beds on the first floor," said Christina. "Okay call Clay Bottom Memorial and start preparing them for more patients, 'Regina said reluctantly.

RALPH WAS PACING back and forth. What in the Hell was going on with his baby girl he wonder. He was about to go out of his mind with speculation. He had spent his life taking care of his family. Ralph did hot like the feeling of hopelessness. Not knowing was not a strong point for him. "Where in the hell is the doctor?"Ralph asked. Liz could feel the hopelessness in Ralph voice. Walking in the hospital, she notices the volume of people in the waiting room seem very congested.

Doctor Patricia Bell examines Annabelle vital signs to see if she had a normal blood pressure. She had come in the hospital with a sixty over forty pressures. How in the world didn't anyone call a doctor?" thought Patricia as she examines Annabelle. Before she could scold anyone she notices most of the people had similar sickness. The illness was familiar to Patricia but she could not put her finger on it. She would have the test results as soon as the computer comes back up.

BRAD SHACK FORD was on his yacht reeling from relaxation. Free away from all worries was the benefits of sailing. Sometimes Brad would go with whatever course the wind took. He enjoy every moment he has to be alone with Mabel his boat. His radio was playing a mix CD he had made. He heard his favorite artist on the radio Rod Stewart. Brad did a little jig, an ancient move of the late eighties he used to get by through social gatherings and on the dance floor. B admired his status in life. He had come a long way from a roll picker in the textile industries so many years ago. He had turned a once seven dollar an hour job into a mass fortune. Shack Ford Industries was just another one of his company that he just happens to pick up. This was the way he had mass his fortune. He would buy other people business through corporate take over's and buying stock from stockholders. Brad was reminiscing back when he first started when he felt his cellar phone pulsating in his pocket. His first response was to wonder what in the hell Joyce, his ex wife wanted, the woman who betrayed him in bed with his cousin on a snowy Christmas Eve many years ago. Time after time, she would call and beg for money to feed her cocaine habit. Sometimes he would indulge her just to hear her voice over at the end of the phone. Somewhere he had the audacity to long for them to get back together again. This time it was not her on the phone. On the phone was Brad Product Control Manager Mark Smith."He don' usually disturb me while I am on vacation," he thought. "Brad we have a problem with lot C", said Mark. "Smith what do you mean problem?" asked Brad. Whatever the problem was head insurance and had good money taking care of it already. "Its lot C," said Mark. At first Brad had no idea to what Mark was talking about then he remember that particular lot Ralph had mention to him about. The lot was using a brand new type of dye that had not passed all the USDA testing. Ralph had warned him about the volubility of the lot. "Brad the chrome dome capsule that contains the dye has rupture," said Mark. "Well, fix it then, "shouted Brad. "We don't know how long it's been leaking or how severe the leak is," said Mark. Brad did not like the sound of this. This had law suit written all over it. Brad remembers that the main pipeline that held the dye in ran beside the city water supply. "We got our men out there as we speak, "said Mark. Brad understood the legalities that could arrive from this situation. Now he planter his next moved as if a person makes a move playing chess. He had to see if there was anything that could t involves him to any negligence, if there was any in this matter. "Brad my men tell me there no way of knowing at this time on how much damage has been done," said Mark. "Who gave the go ahead to run the pipe without the USDA approval?" asked Brad. "You did," said Mark. It seem like all Brad did these days was signing forms for this and that. Perhaps he probably did sign something that gave permission to go ahead but only by sheer exhaustion however, the reason he had to fixed the situation and clear his involvement. It did not take genesis to figure out. There was poison slowly seeping William's Town water supply. "Mark get my people together we are going to have a meeting today ASAP!" yelled Brad.

In life, you do not always get what you want. Sometimes you have to realize the fact that it is what it is. This was what Kim had to come to terms with. She still had her position as file clerk and sometimes that sorry tail Melvin. Kim decided not to ever have dependence in another man She did not expect anything from him and he never promises her anything either. "Deidre pick your toys off this floor," Kim shouted. Now, walking with a limp after twisting her ankle, she bends down to remove the toys out of her way. "Melvin sit your lazy behind down and put that toy down," shouted Kim. Melvin did not like it when Kim yelled at Deidre. Kim His and her dislike Melvin attempt to spoil Deidre "If I tell her to do something I mean for her to do it," Kim said. "Anyway why you aren't looking for work or something, "said Kim. She knew ever since Melvin sprang his ankle he would be no better for work. It seemed not only Melvin dream went up in smoke but also Kim's Of course she blame Melvin but she kind of felt guilty for the resentment she had for him. She defiantly did not want any advice from him especially her children. "You act like I don't have say around my own kids, let me help," said Melvin. "Help help nigger you say help around here again I'm going to help your ass out the door!"Kim shouted. "Kim my disability will soon kick in soon and I promise you will get yours," said Melvin. "I should a done had it," said Kim. Kim had all of this held inside of her. Not even caring anymore what Melvin did or not do. For all she was concern her future was with Ralph and now she was going through the aftermath of the jilted lover. At times Kim felt fortunate. This should have been enough for her and it would have if not for the one percent of bitterness. The contempt she had for Liz because Liz had everything she wanted.

MARK SMITH WAS going through his roster calling up all the maintenance personnel he could mustard. "Ralph, where are you?" he asked. Ralph had left his cell phone number in case of an emergency. Ralph heard his cell phone going off in his inside coat pocket but his focus primarily on Annabelle now. Ralph only took his mind off the situation with Annabelle when doctor Regina walk in the door. Funny how homely she looked way back then and now how attractive she had become. However, Ralph told himself to concentrate on his daughter and he had the best doctor in all William Town. Therefore, there should be no worry. Nevertheless, people were passing out like flies after the fly spray. Ralph was afraid of the answer before he asked the question. However, he waited patiently until she finishes with her assessment on Annabelle. "What's wrong with my daughter doc?" asked Ralph. 'Well Mr. Barns,' said Patricia. 'Please call me Ralph," said Ralph. "Look here Mr. Barns the test results are back," said Patricia. "Yes please tell me what is wrong," pleaded Ralph. "Thallium poison was found in your daughter's bloodstream," said Patricia. 'What kind of poison is that?" asked Ralph. "It can be a form of rat poison that can be submitted individually but yours is not the only case," said Patricia. "How in the world did she get dye poison?" asked Ralph. "I am not saying rat poison was the substance found in the body but the chemical makeup consist of the atomically build up," said Patricia. She began to walk out of the room when she stop suddenly and turn around. "Yours is not our only case Ralph, "said Patricia. "What do you mean?" ask Ralph. "An epidemic," said Patricia. Ralph had completely ignored his phone vibrating in his pocket. He flipped his phone over to answer it. "Hello," said Ralph. Mark Smith answers on the other end. "We got a problem and we need you over here fast," said Mark. "I am at the hospital with my daughter," said Ralph. "You will be brief when you get here," said Mark. Ralph was confused with Mark. Because he would not be so vague with detail and he sounded like he was worried."My daughter could be poison." Said Ralph 'Yeah I know and we probably had something to do with it,' said Mark. Ralph slam down his phone and told Liz he had to go. He did not know who or whom ass he had to kick. Ralph guaranteed he was going to find out what Mark talking about... On his way over to the plant was all he could think about was what Mark said. What did he mean? What in the Hell was going on in William Town? People were getting sick around the town like a small plague gone out of control. Now Annabelle his baby girl was ill. The car veer off the road as Ralph drove carelessly. Ralph manages to fish tail the car back on the road again. Ralph did not like not knowing things. This made him frustrated about everything. He flipped open his phone to call Liz. He had to see if Annabelle had gotten any worse. "Baby how is she doing?" ask Ralph. "She is almost out of the woods, "said Liz. Ralph could hear the calmness in her voice that made him relax. "The doctor said that her fever has broken and she has taken a turn for the good, "said Liz. Ralph composes himself and prepares himself for the meeting. He must have been speeding because he was ten minutes early. When he got in the building, he could hear Brad yelling and slamming furniture. "Somebody must really mess up, "Ralph thought. He crept close to the door to hear what was going on. He came to a complete stop when he heard Brad shouted aloud that he was ruin.

"Look Smith you are my eyes and ears around this place!" shouted Brad. All the members at the meeting feared for their jobs. Ralph finally walks in the room and everything got quiet. "Well I am happy Ralph for gracing us your appearance, "said Brad.

KATRINA ROSS WALKS in Regina office to take a break from the floor. She had not seen that many sick people together at one place

The last patient that came in was an old elderly woman. Patricia did not think this patient was going to last through the night. The patient name was Maggie Stokes. Patricia kept walking back and forth to her room all through the night. "Doctor, did we get a call from the CDC?" asked Katrina. "Yes we did, "answer Patricia. "I think they will shut the whole town down, "said Patricia. "Good we need to get a hand on this crisis, "said Katrina. "I don't know of anything good that'll come from this, God knows we need to find an answer to this problem, "said Regina. She looked on upon her latest patient whose pulse was becoming weaker by the minute. Regina went back into the 1computer room to get the latest data information. It seems like every one that lives in or by William's Town had similar symptoms. Regna waited patiently for more data when Katrina walk in. 'The patient in 311 is getting weaker," said Katrina. Regina just shook her head in frustration. Never before have had she felt this helpless."I know that this illness is similar to rat poison, "said Patricia. The information that Regina was waiting for finally came in.

Liz was standing over Annabelle when Patricia walks in. Patricia was pleases with Annabelle's condition. "Her body is fighting the poison,' said Patricia. How did she get this?"Liz asked. 'We don't know right now but we will find out," said Patricia. All of the tests show Lead Red dye deposits in all of her patients. Patricia spotted her assistant across the hall. "Excuse me Mrs. Barnes I'll be right back," Patricia said. Patricia went over to Katrina and was shock from the news she heard. However, it somehow made sense. "Doc it looks like the CDC had a message for the town of William

Town, "Katrina said. ' What is the message?" Patricia asked. "The water, everybody must boil their drinking water, they think everybody is getting sick through their water supply," Katrina said. Patricia was wondering what the town was up against. There at times the crisis would appear to get better like Annabelle's case. However, everyone prayed for Maggie Stokes.

BRAD PACED BACK and forth in the boardroom thinking what he would say next. Up until this point, he thought he had been upfront with board members. He had to find a solution to get him out of this situation. He was not going down alone. Defiantly some heads was going to rolled other than his. "Sir our lawyer's say we are cover from all the damage in the city," said Henry Harris, the productivity manager. Brad did not know how reliable his lawyers were and he was not putting all his hope in them. "Gentlemen we are not negligence, "said Brad. This negligence could cost him and his company millions. "Ralph you can come in here and kindly explain to me how I authorize lot C," said Brad. Ralph remembers telling Brad to be careful with that particular lot. Now was not the time for him to act as if he had amnesia. "Brad I need to holler at you for a second "said Ralph. He was feeling like a cage animal about to be hem up in a trap. It did not take a genius to figure out what Brad was trying to do. Brad was about to play the blame game and Ralph could smell bullshit a mile away. "Everyone take a five minute brake", said Brad. Ralph, he thought was one of his best employee and a good friend but he was not expendable. "Damn it Ralph it was you who gave me the okay to proceed with that lot," shouted Brad. Ralph did not give Brad any confirmation notices. "Look Ralph what you are saying is ludicrous!" Ralph shouted. "Isn't this the confirmation letter?" Barney asked. Ralph looked at the paper Brad was holding and it looks legitimate. However, it was not his signature. "Look R aleph I trusted your judgment as a mechanic and now the whole city is on my ass!"Brad shouted. "Brad this is not my signature," Ralph said. "It came from your office!" Brad shouted. The letter did come from his office but it was not suppose to. Who in their right mind would break into his office to violate confidential material such as this? "Ralph this is your letter head, "Brad said. "Yeah but how, "Ralph stumbled. "Hand me your keys, I have to let you go, "said Brad. Ten years of good service gone out of the window just like that. Who had set him up Ralph wondered. He just did not know whom. In addition, how did they do it? When he got in front of the building, he thought of whom. "Kim", he said. She was the only one who had access to his important documents and the only person who would love to see him harm. With that thought Ralph march back up to Brad office. Brad was still in his chair when Ralph came in. Brad jumped up not knowing what to expect from Ralph. "Now look Ralph you screw up, it's over, "said Brad. " IT's was not me it was Kim we had an affair, "said Ralph. "What are you talking about Barns?" Brad asked. Ralph had kept his affair with Kim a secret. He had kept their relationship that way because he fears of losing his job and all of the promotions "That's the most despicable thing I heard of Barns, "said Brad. "I know it was crazy that is why I ended it, "said Ralph "You mean to tell me I am about to lose millions over a piece of tail!" Brad shouted. Ralph did not want things to spiral like this. However, he would be lucky if he were to keep his job. Since his job and integrity was on the line "That is why we do not do that kind of crap out here Ralph, "said Brad "Okay you weren't careless with the documents but you were negligence in your behavior but I need you here doing your job not her "said Brad. Ralph knew if he were right Kim would not have a job or a home for her kids."Damn Kim what were you thinking about?"Ralph asks himself. Still Ralph could not help but to feel this was his fault. He should not have lead Kim on in to thinking that one day they would marry. Ralph was just learning Kim and he would find out that she was not build like that. "If this is true I'll have to let her go, "said Brad. 'I understand man but she is a single mother that made a mistake, "said Ralph "'I don't know how big of mistake maybe millions of dollars a mistake!"Shouted Brad Ralph turns around and walk out of Brad office. As he walked down the hallway, he could hear Brad shouting, "Millions I tell you millions". Ralph did all he could by trying to get Brad to reconsider Kim position at the plant.

KIM WAS PLANNING to go in to work early that afternoon. She just wanted to get away from Melvin. It seems like all they had in common these days been fighting. "Hush Larry, I told you to shut up!"Kim shouted. How in the Hell did she fall for this cat. "Woman who are you talking to in there and who is the hell is Larry. Melvin asked. The only things Melvin was good at around the house was eating and sleeping.

On the other hand, Melvin was no saint either but only he and Margret knew his or her dirty deed. That night in question, Margret had shown him love. A kind of love he could not have gotten from Kim.

"MISSY LET EVERYBODY know your sister condition, "said Liz. Missy was relieved from worry of the good news. Her sister was coming out of the woods. "Oh yeah Mrs. Goldie called, "said Missy. Liz knew how her friend could be about news caring. Sometimes she would not bother getting the entire facts, just only the juicy parts."Just tell everyone what I said, "Liz told her. "Okay I will, "said Missy. Liz hung up the phone and walked quiet back to Annabel room. Her daughter strength seems to be getting stronger. The night shift nurse walk in behind Liz and adjusted Annabelle breathing tube. Liz notice how quiet it was in the hospital almost eerie even. Liz wondered how many people had died in this building. The quietness gave the building an extra eeriness."Mrs. Barns can I bring you a snack at ten clocks?"The nurse asks. "No thank you I'm fine, "said Liz. She had been at the hospital for eight hours now and her body was beginning to take a toll on her. She had been in a lot in a short period. The people of her town were getting sick for some unknown reason including her daughter. Liz looks at the small chair in Annabelle's room. Liz knew it would be her bed tonight she was determines to see Annabelle through the night until the morning. Liz thought about how bad Ralph look, how deeply concern and hopeless he felt at the sight of his little girl. She loved that man and devoted her entire life to him. Liz just sat down but before she would know it, she would be asleep. Liz had a vision of a dusty dirt road. She took the road to school when she was a little girl. There was a little girl down the road calling her name repeatedly. She felt like she knew this girl. It was Lillian, her childhood friend. The only thing that was weird to her was Lillian had died thirty years ago. Liz rubs her eyes she was shock when she realized who it was. However, how could this be Liz wonder? The girl did not look a day over sixteen as she remembered, the day Lillian was ran over by a school bus. The ethereal figure floated toward her with a ghastly grin on her face. 'What up home slice, "the figure asked? Lillian always uses a greeting with her friends. "Damn living has not been good to you Elizabeth,' Lillian said. She was the leader of Liz childhood girl's group the Cheetah. "I am just playing girl, stop being so thin skin, "said Lillian. Now Liz remembered Lillian dire sense of humor. "Look here Bee I am not alive again, "Lillian said. Liz heart began to pump harder and faster when she realizes she was indeed talking to a dead being. "No I am not dead, however I am here to provide warning, "said Lillian. Liz stood up in earnest and wonder what did Lillian had to warn her about."Look here siesta girl beware of your surroundings this sister is not right in the head. Lillian voice seemed to rise up into a howling pitch." You and your family lives are in danger "said Lillian. Lillian was really being vague with information Liz thought. The road that Liz was standing in seems to disappear and slowly fade away. So did Lillian also but she could hear Lillian in the background chanting beware Elizabeth. The daydream had left Liz fully awake. The night attendant was passing through and seen Liz standing up. "Ma'am is you okay?" she asked. "Oh dear I am fine, "Liz lied. She was not fine. It was not often Liz dreamt about dead people. She was still startled from the warning her childhood friend had given her. Who in the world want to hurt her? When it came to people Liz, enjoy them even down to the littlest of them. However fortunate she thought she was she always was nice to them. When it came to her family, Liz was very protective. She possessed the exploits of a mama pit bull in heat. You just did not mess with her or her family in any kind of way. Liz went in Annabelle's room to check on her. Annabelle was still asleep but it looks like the fever had broken.

M ARK SMITH HAD the task of cleaning out Kim's desk. He understood what it meant when he did this task. He would have to be the one to fire the newly unemployed. Also, give them, the courteous to walk them out the front door. This pertain a lot of cussing and arguing, something Mark usually avoided. He was so busy in his efforts to clean that he did not see Kim standing in the doorway. "It's about time I get moved, "said Kim. "I am sorry Ms. Jenkins you are fire, "said Mark. "Excuse me!" Kim shouted. Here we go again thought Mark. He hated to deliver bad news to people especially someone as fine as Kim looked. "I know Ralph had something to do with this, "said Kim. "Ms. Jenkins I do not have anything to do with it "said Mark. "Yeah I know you just doing your job, "said Kim comically. "Ma'am please follows me, "said Mark. In her mind, she wonders why she put her trust in sorry ass men. Now what was she going to do for her kids. The last thing Social Services need to know is she with no job. When Kim reach the front of the office building where Ralph office was. Kim shook her fist in the air at his door. In anger was all she could feel now. A wave of hatred flowed through her veins. All she could see now was Ralph down fall. Not only was she tired of men, she was tired of life kicking her down. It was time for her to kick back. The reason she was feeling this way was not the loss of her job even though it had something to do with it. It had been months since she had stop taken her Schizophrenic pills and she was feeling a manic episode coming on and a little bird telling her to "choke the bitch". Kim was thinking of away she was going to get even with Ralph. Still she told the bird to shut up. She went to bed with this fool parrot on her bedroom nightstand deliberative on why she should kill. This time life had gone too far and Larry was starting to make sense to Kim. When Kim reached her home in her driveway, she saw an unknown vehicle park there. Kim stopped her car and got out."What are you going to do bitch ask question?"Larry mocked .Before she got to her front door; she heard the sounds that reveal her worst fear. Her sorry behind husband was in there with another woman. Kim crept inside of her house and calmly walked in the kitchen. The noise she had heard had stop. Kim look on her kitchen counter and grab the biggest butcher knife she could find. Kim heard Melvin coming towards the kitchen and she hid in the walk-in closet and waited. Melvin was very thirsty after his morning workout. He had to get the last bit of Kool-Aid in the refrigerator. As he threw back his head to drink then he heard something in the closet. "Damn I know we don't have rats now, "Melvin said. He stops drinking and walk to the closet. If only he known what was on the other end of the closet door, maybe he would not had left his chest so wide open. The butcher knife went through Melvin heart like hot metal going through butter. It happens so fast that Kim did not have time to think. Melvin fell back and hit the floor gurgling in his own blood. Kim step over Melvin dying body and was heading for the door and stop in front of it. "Shut the hell up Larry!" shouted Kim. She shouted and turns around and went back in the kitchen to see Melvin. Kim stood there for a second or two admiring her handy work. She then knelt down and gave Melvin a kiss on his lips. Then she put her hand on the knife handle and plunge it deeply in once more. Next, she snatched the instrument out, ran to the back bedroom, leaped in the air, and landed on her sleeping victim. Kim just started stabbing the poor girl in her sleep. Had the girl had not been asleep Kim probably would have notice her because she saw her face every morning at work. She would have known that the girl in her bedroom was Margret Barns. "Leave me alone Larry!" Kim shouted as she swung in mid air.

IT WAS LATE when Ralph arrives at the hospital. Liz was standing over her child caressing her forehead. Annabelle condition was stable now. Even her breathing had gotten easier. Ralph walks up to her from behind and kisses her on the neck. Liz turned around and hugs him tighter than usual "Ralph what did you mean this was probably your fault?" Liz asks. "Baby it's just a damn mix-up down there at the plant," said Ralph. He continues with his story to Liz leaving out the situation with Kim. The reason why he did not mention her was the possibility of her finding out about Kim and him. To Liz it sounded like her husband was being a fall guy "Ralph you don't make mistakes like that especially a million dollar mistake like that," said Liz. Ralph knew it was not a mistake it was intentional. This was the raft of a scorned woman .Kim had been broken too many times.

BISHOP JACK CLARK was in Maggie Stokes kneeling over bedside. Gertrude Brooks walk in on her old advisory. She wanted to pray along with the bishop. "Gertrude it's good to see you sister, "said the Bishop. "Yeah we need to prey in time of trouble, 'said Gertrude. Now that was what she did. Gertrude would be the first to say, "He without sin cast the first stone". Having come short on all fronts Gertrude would be the first to forgive and understand."Sis is pulling through now, "said the Bishop. Maggie started to moan and turning as if she was trying to get up. "Gertrude go get somebody she trying to awake!" the Bishop shouted. The attendant came in the room just to see what the commotion was. He shock Maggie and she seem to gain consciences.

KIM JENKINS STOPS by Helen Brooke's house to pick up Melvin's kids. She had been helping keeping them because of her work on third shift, no one world keep them. Helen thought this was somewhat strange for Kim to be by this time of day. Deaneries came running out screaming "Kim, bmKim you are here!" she shouted. Helen was concern for Kim to be here and not at work. "Is there anything wrong Kim?"Helen asks. "Wrong oh no I am just taking a brake that's all, "Kim answered. Not mention all the hell she and Larry had committed a few hours ago. "Deuce, Deidra, you all gets in the back seat now, "Kim told them. Helen walks back in her house. She thought that little exchange of words was odd. "Helen, who was that driving out of here like a bat out of hell?" Ella asked. "Oh that Jenkins girl, with her kids, "said Helen. 'Lord knows how I worry about that girl, "Ella said "You know Ella, that girl is kind of odd," Helen chuckle. Both of the two went into the kitchen where Ella had made breakfast.

"**W**HERE ARE WE going Kim?"Denice asked. "Mommy is taking some time off, that's all, "Kim said. 'Kim goes fast!"Deuce shouted. The three year old was thrill with the speed of the automobile going through the curves of that country road. "Deuce, sat your ass down before I get pull over!"Kim yelled. Kim glance at the speedometer, which read 120mph it was sheer anger that made her, go faster. However, when she saw smoke from the hood of her 1964 Chevy station wagon was when she slows the vehicle down. Kim had pushed the car to its manufactory limit. The car coasted down the road where it stopped to the foot of the Blount's Creek Bridge. The car was completely exhausted and so was Kim. She sat there just beating her head against the steering wheel. Nothing in her life seems to go right and now it is worthless. Kim understood that she could never go back. She even thought about turning herself in to the authorities although, by the time she would get out of prison Deidre and Deuce would be grown. There were not many things Kim took pride input being a good mother was one of them. Kim looks at her little darlings and then grabs them by the hand. "Come on children, 'said Kim. Kim took them by the hand and walk on the bridge. When they got to the middle part of the bridge, they stop. "Are we going to go for a swim Kim?"Denise asked. "Yes baby swimming, "Kim said. "Yeah swimming, "shouted Deuce. Kim had reached that point where she realizes now she could never go back. She bent down to pick up Deuce "Hey man let's play a game of who's the best swimmer, "said Kim. "Kim I do not know how, "said Denise 'Oh it is easy just relax yourself, "said Kim. "Leave me now Larry!" Kim shouted. Just as she was picking up a sack of potatoes, Kim threw Melvin babies off the bridge. "Kim, Kim it's cold!" screamed Denise. Kim only stood there listens to the children screams of the cold of the waters. Deuce floated up to the surface couple of times before you did not see his little head anymore. "Help me Kim please!"Denise screamed. Kim only stood there until she could not hear her daughter screams anymore. Kim felt deep in her heart that no one could give her kids the love she could give them. By that fact, they were better off dead. So the voice in her head told her. Kim parked her car way behind the guard shack at Shack Ford Industries; she had hoped not to discover. Instead, her plan was to try to fool Ralph into meeting her alone where she could nosh her revenge. She figure Ralph would be usually at his office and normally she would just walk in his office but now she did not have an ID badge to show the guard at the gate. Bending down behind her car she crept very carefully and quietly she admire her stealthiest. Her goal was to pounce on Ralph when he came out. However all her plans change when she felt the cold metal of the nightstick ridding up against her skirt. 'May I help you madam?"Bud Foreman asked. Kim was not in shock because of his hesitation she figures him as an individual to be up to no-good. "Sir I lost my keys somewhere out here, do you think you could help me find them?"Kim asked the guard. Bud Forman almost laid on the ground in his attempt to help the woman to find her keys. "A pretty young and helpless, defenseless woman, should not be out here this late looking for her keys, "said Bud. Had he paid attention to the butcher knife Kim held in her hand half as much as he did her behind Bud Forman would have made it home to his wife that afternoon? Instead, all he felt was the cold steal of the blade going through his throat. Kim ran through the thick blood that oozes down the street and in the water drain. The adrenaline that she felt was better than any stimulating sex she ever had. Again, that was what the voice inside of her head was trying to convince her. Killing was really good.

CARLOS CHAVEZ WAS moping around the house all that morning. He was sulking because he had not heard from Margret all day. He had no reason not to trust her but he felt like something in their relationship was wrong it even got to the point where she was not answering his calls. Carlos thought this would be the women of his dreams. He wishes they had not got in a fight the night she met his mom. She had not answered his calls since. Carlos walked in the living room to check his message. He had three messages, one from his friend Bubba and one from his mother and a bill collector for his big screen TV set. However, there was no message from Margret. When he calls her phone all he got was the leave your name, answer the beep message. The telephone rang and Carlos heart beat with a sign of relief. He picked the phone up thinking it would be Margret on the other end. "Carlos, where is my big head sister?"Missy asked. Carlos heart began to descend to the bottom of his heart. He was feeling with confusion and worry than anger. "What do you mean?"Carlos asked. "I mean where my sister is, "Missy asked. He wonders where in the hell she was. Now his heart was beating faster and faster with anxiety "What do mean she isn't home?"Carlos asked. "We haven't seen her in two days, "said Missy. "I have not talk to her in three, "said Carlos. Missy was alarm now because her sister was always the responsible one. Missy did not know where Margret was. What did Carlos do to her sister to make her this mad?

BISHOP JACK CLARK had just arrived to the hospital to prey for his most loyal church member. He had not been there for ten minutes when Gertrude Brookes walk in."Thank you Jesus another prayer partner," Bishop Clark said. "We need your help father God, "Gertrude chanted. "Yes father, stop by here now if you will, yes right now Jesus, "Bishop Clark prayed. They would have made members at Morning Glory proud with their performance they were giving to Maggie. Someone who did not know any better would think the dead were trying to be raise. Bishop the doctor said the water had become contaminated," Gertrude said "Is that right; I thought they check for things like that, "said Bishop Clark. "Yeah they are supposing to, "said Gertrude."That should be a multimillion-dollar lawsuit, "said Bishop Clark. He had studied law in collage. "Wall in that case I am thinking about checking myself in, "Gertrude chuckle. They decided to go to the break room because both of them had work up an appetite. "Yes I tell you somebody messed up pretty bad, "Bishop Clark said. "Um hum I know that is right, "said Gertrude. Bishop Clark saw Maggie's physician standing across from him. "Gertrude, excuse me I am about to ask her about Maggie's condition," the Bishop said. The doctor looked exhausted from lack of sleep. "Pastor, Maggie has come a long way from the poison infection but I am afraid she is not out of the woods yet, "Doctor Bell said. 'Maggie is one of my most faithful members and I will be praying for her every day, "Bishop Clark said. Regina was trying her best to be attentive to what the Bishop was saying to her but between fatigue and lack of interest. Her focus was containing this poison in William Town and stopping any more out breaks. "Excuse me I am about to go check on her right now, you can come with me maybe she can recognize your voice and come around from her sleep," said Dr. Regina. The traffic at Pitt Memorial seems to decelerate and most of the patients were recovering from their sickness. Regina felt the worst was over. The Barn's daughter was cognitive and in good shape. She felt a certain nub against her shoulder it was her assistant Katrina. "Hey doc I am on brake, ok doc?" Katrina asked. "Fine, you deserve it," said Dr. Regina. "Come on children let's go and give the almighty an almighty praise," Bishop Clark said. The three of them held hands in the middle of the hallway and gave praise and thanks.

MISSY PACED BACK and forth in her room. She had called all of her friends but no one seen hair or tail of Margret. This was strange because Margret would usually be the person who was responsible. Missy remembered a conversation she was having with Egypt about how possessive her boyfriend was. Missy wonders if Carlos had those tendencies. The more she thought about it the more she worried. She called the hospital to tell her mother her concern. Liz answered her phone at first sleepy eyed but then hysterical when she heard of Margret's disappearance. "What do you mean you haven't seen her?" Liz asked. "Mom I thought she was with Carlos all this time," Missy said. "Look me and your father is calling the authorities," Liz told her. Ralph had the feeling of what next. What curse had he stumbled on, he wondered? Something that seems to involved his entire family.

SHERIFF DEE COATES had just joined the department just little over two years. She received her basic training in Macon, Georgia. When the position came open in William Town, North Carolina, she jumps for the assignment. She like how quiet William Town was. Crime seems to be nonexistence. The town was quiet and safe especially for her sixteen-year-old daughter Patrice. Ray Macaroni the department dispatcher "Dee, we just got a call for a missing person," said Ray. At last her first missing person case, Dee thought. "Who's missing and how long?"Dee asked. "Ralph and Liz Barn's daughter, Margret, "said Ray. "When we're she last seen and who with?"Dee asked. "Her sister Missy, told her parents that she thought Margret Was with her boyfriend Carlos Chavez two days ago, "said Ray. "Let us go and pay Mr. Chavez a visit, "Dee said. Even though Carlos did not have a record he was automatic assume suspect. Why, was it because he was the last to see Margret, yeah according to Missy he was.

MARK SMITH WAS in his office finishing some last assignments for the day when he barely notice the clock on his wall in his office. It was 5minutes passed ten pm.; it was pass time for Bud Forman, the security guard to let him out of the parking lot. He should have been by his office at 9: 30p.m. to remind him of the time.

The air was so thin Mark had difficulty breathing. The back of the parking lot once was fill with hectic machinery during the day now seem like a bomb out field where lost souls reside within. Mark clutched his briefcase tighter and tighter as he got to his car. Mark fumbles with his flashlight and his keys. Then eventually dropping hi flash light which rolled under his car. "Damn what 'sin the hell is wrong with you man?"He muttered aloud to himself. There was a sigh of relief when he finally sat in his car. Although Mark was safe in his car, he sat there for a couple of minutes. Had he not been sitting down he would have stood up when the butcher knife blade came through the seat and into his heart. Mark could not even scream instead he died with his mouth frozen with the words why Kim!

CARLOS HEARD A knock on his door. Again, he hopes it was Margret. The sheriff department, Ray Macron and sheriff

Dee Coates stood at the door. Carlos was afraid that there had been an accident or some other dreadful news. The law never stops at his door. "Are you Carlos Chavez?" Ray Macron asked, "Yes I am he, "Carlos answered. "We need to ask you some question, may we come in?"Ray asked. "Come on in," Carlos said. Sheriff Coates walked in behind Ray Macron and began question Carlos about Margret's whereabouts. "Chavez, I understand that you know Margret?'"Dee asked. "We were lovers, "said Carlos. "What do you mean were?"Sheriff Coates asked. "We had an argument and I haven't seen her since Friday, "said Carlos. "Carlos, her family tells us that it is highly unusual for Margret to go missing this long without a phone call, letting everybody know she is alright," Ray said.

KIM'S LITTLE 110POUND small frame body climb over from the back seat of Mark's car and hoist Mark over her shoulders as if he was a sack of flour. This time she was going to do the escorting. "Excuse me sir but you have to leave this parking lot, hey I'm just doing my job," Kim laughed as she drugged him where she had put Bud Forman. She had come out here tonight to get even with Ralph. She thought his fault to herself. However, what about all of the other unnecessary killings who fault were those? In Kim' fanatical state of mind everything was justified. Nevertheless, what about her babies did they deserve to be murdered? In Kim mind she did what a good parent supposed to do, she took care of her kids and put them in a better place. Kim understood that she was on a path that she could never get off. Kim was on the run and things could never be the same ever again. "Look at you bitch I told you to listen to me and handle the shit the way I told you" "Shut up Larry!" shouted Kim to her imaginary friend

EVEN THOUGH SHE had been on this path for years it seem it all started with an innocent spade card game with her older brother Reggie. Kim had always looked up to her big brother but he would always be the winner in any game she played. This continues until one Sunday afternoon. They had started out that morning sitting down together to table unto a big breakfast that their mother Big Heavy made. It was her mother's Sunday mornings breakfast, which usually entails grits, eggs, and red sausage, and bacon and cheese biscuits. That particular day proceed as usually until that particular card game. For some reason Reggie was on his game and skill in comebacks or "dozens": slang for trash talk. This was something Kim's have always done since she was able to talk and so Reggie only he was better at it then her. It seem like Reggie although funny, even hilarious, seemed to get personal and more personal and meaner. Reggie had not realize that he had hurt his sister feelings. All he was doing was just having fun, at her expense however, but only in fun. Reggie jumped up in the air and laughs very hard after telling his best joke he had ever told about his sister. After a second, he looked around for his sister to high five her for his humor. Instead, Kim had left the room, the game, with her whole hand dispose on the table. He herds Kim in the kitchen going through the draws. "Stop eating, come out you greedy strumpet," laughed Reggie. Reggie could not understand why his baby sister had stopped commenting on his style. 'Come on here girl it's your turn!" Reggie yelled. Reggie looked behind him and saw Kim standing there with kitchen butcher knife in her hand. "Look Kim don't cut all of Mama Pie, I'm telling, "Reggie said. "Tell this," said Kim. Kim only reacted with her emotions. Without giving a solitary thought, she plunged the butcher knife in Reggie's heart and there he lay on the kitchen table bleeding like a stuck hog. Fortunately, it was not Reggie's time to meet his maker because he nearly bleeds to death. However, for Kim sake there was not that many places you could send a problem child in those days. Society was not that educated on the mental state of individuals. She ended up at the Little's Honey Academy for collared Girls until she was eighteen. After that, she went to Dotty Dikes Mental Health Center. Kim lived there until she was thirty. She had met with Lillian Williams during that time a license physiologist who took an interest in Kim's case. "She is suffering from all of the delusional disorders, erotomatic, grandiose, jealous, persecutory, romantic and mixed," Lillian said, murmuring to herself as went over Kim file.

"Day one subject asked why she stabbed her brother. Subject responded that her pet parrot told her to do it. A bird she lost when she was ten years old. Now the bird acts like her conscious when she about to do wrong." Lillian was fascinated with the episode that Kim experience without her medication. "Day two subject swears she doesn't want to listen to the bird but the bird has a filthy mouth and be threatening her. The subject tried to resist sometimes but Larry, her dead bird never seemed to care for Reggie. The subject said that she believe the bird came back to protect her". Dr. Williams classified Kim Bowen highly dangerous, highly risk, and psychotic episodes with lack of medication. This woman should never see the light of day. She had a wide range of question to ask Kim when she saw her during her 1:00clock session. Lillian order a lunch plate at 11:00clock that morning because she was planning to eat an early lunch. She was shock to hear the facility siren going off. Lillian intestinally ran to lock her room door because this was part of her training. Her door swung open and it was hospital security. "Dr. Williams it's your patient Kim Bowen, she has killed and escapes. The orderly found dead in the broom closet .He lay on the floor with his pants downswing around his knees in his own pool of blood. Apparently, he had let his guard down one too many times.

"Ha ha, I know he shame", said Larry. "Shut up Larry and stop talking to me!" Kim yelled, talking to her imaginary pet. "Who are you talking to bitch it's your fault in the first place, you should have killed the bitch in the first place we would've never have been here" "Please shut up before I," stammer Kim. "Before what bitch, you can't kill me now you shut the fuck up!" Kim ran down the alley and hid inside of the dumpster and escape.

Lillian walked back in her office with the head of Little Honey Academy security Patrick Brian. "Tell me what are we dealing with doc? Patrick asked. "Well Kim is a very trouble woman but now it's no telling now what she going to do without her meds, "said Lillian.

PATRICK HAD HIS office to spread the news to the surrounding counties. "Red alert, red alert, we have an extremely dangerous mentally ill female escapee!" Patrick shouted. He understood it would be him and his entire department was negligence for Kim's carnage. Patrick had one guard down a he knew if Kim was not stop it would be more deaths. He walk up to the map on his wall. He pinpointed three different towns Kim could have escaped. The towns were Edwards, Bell Arthur and Williams Town. Patrick expected Kim to find refuge in the town of Williams Town.

Kim did find refuge; she had answered an ad on the internet looking for companionship and a mother for his kids. The man describe himself as an ex jock and was recently widowed. The man introduces himself as Melvin Jenkins. Kim thought this would be the opportunity to change her identity. Melvin took her in his home the very minute he laid eyes on her.

IT HAD BEEN a long night at the hospital where Liz toss and turn all night. She looked across from where she was laying to see Ralph still asleep. The night nurse was in and out her room giving her updates on Annabelle's progress. Today she woke up with greater hope for her daughter. Ralph was now waking up. Stretching and yawning letting the world know that he was up. "Good morning baby damn I am hungry," Ralph said. Liz looked at Ralph with admiration because she had so much love in her heart. "Baby why don't you go downstairs and get some coffee," Liz said, she did not have to say this twice because he was famished. "Honey tilled me what do you want?"Ralph asked. "Bring me back a bagel and some coffee, "Liz said. "Ok baby, "said Ralph.

MISSY WAS IN mopping around her house it did not seem the same without her sisters there. They always kept the place lively,and Anne belle made sure of that. Missy herd the phone rang . Missy was hoping it was her mother telling her some good news about her sister. Instead, it was her mother's best friend Gerdine. In the past she had not been that fun of her because she though that Gerdine ran her mouth too much. "Hello, no they have not got back it, but I will let you know something when I know something," Missy told her. Missy made it a point not to convey to much information to Geraldine she would have your business in the streets before you knew what was going on. Missy did not even think Geraldine was sincere at all just was nosy for the latest juicy news.

"Wake up dear Maggie May '. Maggie rubbed her eyes still asleep she thought because she swore she heard her dead husband Sal voice waking her up. "I was worried about you Maggie," Sal said. Maggie stood up in shock. She could not believe it, Sal been dead for ten years. "How in Jesus name can you be talking to me, unless it's my time?"Maggie asked. "Relax Maggie it's not your time, "said Sal. "Where am I?"Maggie asked. "You are not where you think you are, "said Sal. For a moment, Maggie thought she was going to meet her maker. It did not past logic for her to be speaking to her dead husband. "Then tell me where am I at, "Maggie said. "You are not either here nor there you are in limbo, "said Sal. It felt strange talking to her ex-better half. That is probably why she did not ask him if he made it to heaven or not. "Maggie around here is like 1966 all over again we even got Sam Cooke down here, "said Sal. Maggie remembers that year very well especially the day on May 26 1966, she and Sal was married. Sal kept looking at Maggie as if he had forgotten to tell her something. "Maggie, you are much needed in this town, "said essage that came from Sal.. Maggie did not think so because everyone seems to be concern with him or her. Nobody seems to notice her anyway. She did not know what Sal was saying. "Your time is not now, these people need you, "said Sal. Maggie thought that Sal voice was getting weaker and weaker. Infract Sal had faded away and Maggie was opening her eyes to Doctor Bell, her friend Gertrude Brookes and Bishop Clark. Maggie was still groggy from the anesthesia but mentally she was trying to understand the message that came from Sal. She dud remember how Bishop Clark preach at Sal funeral and how he performed at her setting-up by letting his hands going secretly everywhere undetected. Bishop Clark gave a new meaning to laying hands on the sick. The rest of Dr .Bell's patients recover from that poison out break where no one died and no one was charge.

SHERRIFF COATES WAS determine to find Margret Barns alive and well. She thought perhaps,maybe it was just a jealous lover spat. What ever the reason why the girl had been missing seem suspicious and carlos look supicous as hell.

"What mood was your girlfriend in sir when you last saw her?" Deidra asked. Carlos thought the law should be out looking for Margret instead question him with mundane questions. 'When I last saw Margret was Saturday, when I got off from work, "Carlos told Deidra. "So you are telling me, Margret wasn't upset when she left you?"Deidra asked again, now getting aggravated with Carlos. They had been grilling Carlos for almost an hour and they had no answers. "Chavez something here doesn't smell like it's supposed to "said Ray. "Yes, it is stinking to hog manure hell, "Deidra added. Carlos realized now the questions seem to be pointing a finger towards him. "Where were you yesterday when someone reported her missing?"Ray asked. "I was here, sleep, "said Chavez. "Which is it, here or sleep?"Ray asked. Chavez started to realize now, he was the primary suspect of his girlfriend missing person case. "Chavez what argument, if any did you and Margret have son?"Ray asked. Chavez knew deep down in his heart that he did no wrong yet still he felt like a guilty crook. The questions about the time of day were what he took for granted. He did not write down every single detail of the day and felt that he did not need to. Deidra decided to follow up on more leads elsewhere. 'Please, Mr. Chavez lets us know any news on Ms. Barns please lets us know and do not leave town without notifying us first, "Deidra said.

Deidra Coates had just sat down in her recliner from a hard day of work. She notices that her sixteen year old was not home. She looked at her watch to make sure of the time. 'Lord knows that child is going to be the death of me, "Deidra thought to herself. It was near eight o clock when Patrice came in. Deidra rarely yelled at her daughter but giving that she was an hour late and a missing girl was not found Deidra ripped at her."Upstairs to bed young lady!" shouted Deidra Patrice was finally coming out of her shell. This made Deidra happy because Patrice had missed old friends. She seemed to be more active now and lately talking more on the phone. "I don't know who you think you are coming in this time of day!"Deidra yelled. "Mom it wasn't my fault, "Patrice pleaded. "Look saves it, "Deidra said, that usually means shut up

Deidra had walked back into her kitchen when she wondered if Patrice had eaten anything today."Girl what did you eat?" Dee asked. "Mom I had two burgers, I am full, "Patrice said. "Tricia you have to be more responsible than that," "Deidra said. "But it was not my fault," Patrice said. The look on Dee face made Patrice retire for the night. She knew that it would be useless to keep up with that rhetoric. Deidra was going over her notes for today. The Barns missing person case was her first. She did not wanted to let any rug left unturned. Since Deidra lived here, the town of Williams Town had been calm. However, in the last couple of weeks things have not been the same. Was all these unusual infrequent a mere coincidence? What were strange to her were how small Williams Town was. Nevertheless, no one saw Margret in this link of time. The phone wrung louder than usual at 9:00pm that night. It was her partner Ray with news she had been fretting since the beginning of this case. "Deidra come down here, we got a double homicide, "said Ray. Deidra got her things and yelled at Patrice that she had an emergency. The roads were block off when she arrived at the crime scene. "Deidra the missing Barns girl was found dead with 36 stab wounds "said Ray. "Who is the other victim?"Deidra asked. "The decease is Melvin Jenkins, Kim Jenkins ex-husband, live in boyfriend, "said Ray. This was going to be Deidra first murder case and she knew this was going to be a long night. "Deidra, the medical examiner said that the Barns girl probably died on the fourth stab wound, "said Ray. "Whoever did this was mad as hell, "said Deidra. "Yes the other victim looked like his death was by surprise but sir there was no break in. "He probably knew his killer than, "said Deidra. "Good deduction, "said Ray. "I want to talk to these victims close of kin, "said Deidra. "We got that Chavez in there crying his eyes out like a baby, "said Ray. Deidra thought about Patrice. She knew that Patrice was old enough to handle herself without her supervision for a couple hours. This was going to be a long night not only she had to question Chavez whereabouts she also had to deal with the Barns family and inform of their lost. "Ray, what do you think?" Deidra asked. "Well he isn't talking at least not without his lawyer," said Ray. Chavez's lawyer was a young 28-year-old Afro-American woman name Varian Moore. Fresh out of law school both her and Deidra was virgins in their fields. "Are you holding my client?" Varian asked. "No, we just need a statement from him telling us of his whereabouts, "Deidra said. 'Well excuse me so I have council with my client," said Varian. Dee walks back to her truck where Ray was waiting for her. "'Ray I want you to send two of your best officers to go down and console the Barns family, 'said Deidra.

Maggie woke up this morning with energy she had not felt in years. She was ready to leave the hospital and felt that her time had come to help and warn her community. It was time for her act on her instincts, her woman intuition, her feeling to warn her community of the upcoming evil her late husband Sal, had warn her about. All of her life Maggie had never thought of herself to be psychic but she never had a near death experience until now. The poison likes to have killed her. But she manage to walk away from death and now her body had become an instrument from the spirit world. Maggie felt a certain responsibility to find this sick individual Sal had warned her of. Maggie thought that the killer was still hiding from society waiting to pounce on her next victim. "Nurse I got to go", Maggie pleaded. Katrina Ross was please with Maggie condition but it was not up to her it was up to Regina to make that decision. 'We will see what the doctor say", Katrina said. 'Well I need to speak to her immediately!" shouted Maggie. "What is your need?"Regina asked, who had been standing near the door way."I need to go home doc." Maggie said. "Well your vital signs are better than they were when you came in here and I think you are able to go but take it easy when you get home, "Regina told her. "Thank you doc I will take it easy," said Maggie. Even though she had no intentions to be still.

Deidra Coates was at her office waiting to hear of Kim Jenkins whereabouts. Her entire department was on the lookout for this psychotic killer. Accordingly, to her clock on her desk it was 5:45, she was running late tonight. Deidra did not like working all day without checking on Patrice . Even though Patrice was old enough Deidra did not like the fact that Patrice was on her way to become a grown woman . When the phone ranged she was prepare to say to Patrice that she would soon be off. Instead, it was Maggie on the other end of phone. "Yes sheriff I think a crime is about to be committed tonight," said Maggie." Mrs. Stokes who are you talking about?" asked Deidra. "I believe you know the lady,'said Maggie. "Maim I am sorry but you are talking in riddles, "said Deidra. "The woman you are looking for is about to strike again,"said Maggie. Deidra listens to the urgent cy in the voice of the lady from the phone. She have never believed in physics although she have herd of them in solving many different other cases while during her training. Although this was the beginning of her case Deidra was willing weigh in all types of solutions including physics to help her to solved this case. "Mrs. Stokes I have all of men out looking for Kim Jenkins," Deidra said. "You are looking for a woman, but you need to be on the lookout for the evil entity that sit on this woman on her shoulders," Maggie Stokes. With this information, Deidra though she was talking to a crazy woman and she also thought she did not have time to listen to someone who probably down the road of needing some professional help. "Thank you, Mrs. Stokes we will be on the lookout," said Deidra rushing to get off the phone. Deidra did not have anything against older people in fact she appreciated the help this woman was trying to give. Physics she thought was just a little bit far fetch. "Look sheriff, I believe your killer will strike tonight," said Mrs. Stokes.

K IM JENKINS WAS crouch on the floor hiding in Ralph office. In her mind she thought it had come to this. Ralph had lied to her and played with her emotions. Ralph had given her an unrealistic hope. Killing Ralph would be just another chapter with her unfavorable experiences with men. Kim thought back she was thirteen when her mother and father spited up. During this time, Kim was having difficulty transition into womanhood. Times was hard for her mother it was not easy raising three kids and a mortgage all by herself. Sometimes Kim mother accepted the help from her ex brother in law Lawrence. Uncle Lawrence would at times, check in on the family. At different times, he would pay a utility bill or bring some groceries when there were not any. During these time mother was at the factory working, most of the time working over time. Lawrence would find he handy to be there to watch the kids for her mother. However, the only thing Lawrence was watching was Kim's boobs that were just starting to develop beyond Kim's control. Lawrence would pretend that he was concern about his brother's kid's welfare but instead he was only biding his time to get Kim alone and have his way with her young vulnerable body. The time that he was waiting for finally came. It was a typical night like any other night where mother had to go to work. Kim was the only child at home Reggie and Randy had decided to spend the night with their friends. Kim decided that it would be her night to watch the Waltons , her favorite tv show. Usually that would be an argument between her and Reggie since he could not stand theWaltons. Tonight it seem kind of erre with being alone with Uncle Lawrence. Tonight he seemed to act creepy in a touchy, feely kind of way. When she was cleaning, her dish he had came up behind her and message her neck and complement her on how grown up she was becoming. She had even notice the sound in his voice had lower from his normal voice. Kim shook from his touch in the past she had enjoy an embrace from her uncle but these days it seemed like her breast was getting in their way. Kim went inside the living room hoping it would be soon for mother to come home. For a while there was silence in the house beside the television. Then all at once it happen Uncle Lawrence grabbed her and dragged her in the hallway and force all 265 pounds on her. He raped her right there in the middle of the hallway. When he was finish, he threatened her not to tell her mother or anyone else. Kim went in the bathroom to wash off what had happen to her. She felt filthy and did not care what Lawrence had worn she was telling mother everything. When she had finish taking her shower she had realize her mother was home. Kim was on her way to her mother's room when she heard her mother's moan "Oh Lawrence". Kim turned around and went back into her room. She realized that it would be hopeless telling her mother anything. This was Kim's introduction to man hood. There was no wonder why Kim had such haltered toward any man. There was still a side to her that needed love. Larry had told her that was bullshit,"You don't need anybody bitch", that was what he would tell her. During that year, Lawrence met a premature death. It seem like he had fallen asleep behind the wheel of his 1972 Ford truck on his way to work. The corner stated that his death was the result of a heart attack. Which was somewhat odd for a thirty-three year-old? Kim realizes that sometimes in life you could get away with murder if you took your time and plan it. Mother seemed to be in shock of Lawrence death and Father never even knew why Mother was poignant but Kim knew but she went on as if she did not know why. Kim founded out that she was very good in hiding things to herself. All she need now was a clear head and fewer comments from that wicked malevolent beast. The floor in Ralph office was cold and hard to Kim's knees and elbow but she knew it be worth it in the end. She was going to make Ralph pay for it all tomorrow morning when he came in to work. "You should kill all of them Kimberly, all of them Ralph and his fat tail wife Liz," taunted the beast inside of Kim's head. "Shut up Larry, I know who to kill and who need my vengeance,!" shouted Kim at her imaginary friend. "Oh shut up bitch I am the real killer," Larry said. Kim put both of her hands on both o her ears and tried to concentrate on the upcoming events, Ralph demise.

RALPH HAD NOT planned his weekend spending at the hospital. However, his daughter Annabelle life was at stake. Throughout the night, she seemed to improve. Ralph wanted his marriage to do the same. Every man ,Ralph thought, have to know his limitations. Ralph had to know if he still had it, the looks and skill to pull woman. However, infantile that thought was Ralph had fun with Kim. Still he was glad the fling was over. Ralph realized what he had with Liz and all the loving in the world was not worth enough to lose his wife. Now he was determine to be a better husband. As he had this thought inside of his head, Ralph squeezes Liz. Ralph held Liz even tighter through the night.

When Ralph got down stairs, he was approach by two detectives who had been waiting for him. "Mr. Barns we have some bad news to give you," Detective Blount. Ralph mind have been on his baby girl Annabelle and her health. He was not even ready for the news he was to get from the detectives.

From the look on the men face he knew it was far serious than normal. The look on their faces told Ralph that the outcome was helpless. "Sir we have bad news concerning your daughter Margret. "Sir my name is Sergeant Crocker and my partner Detective Davisson," said Frank Crocker. "I think you need to sit down so you will be prepared for this sad news we have to tell you, "Detective Davisson. The detective continue to explain to Ralph that his missing daughter seem to have been caught up in a deadly love triangle and has been murder and the suspected killer may have been a jealous wife name Kim Jenkins. "Mr. Barns we understand she worked under you," said Sergeant Crocker.

The news evaporated what energy he had left inside of him. He did not even have enough energy to scream but Liz had enough for the both of them. All through the night and early in the wee hours of the morning Liz scream. Ralph comforted his wife all through the night because that was what Liz needed. In fact, that was what he needed also. He decided that if they were going to make it , it would be them pulling together. Ralph held Liz tightly however it did not erase the fact that his daughter was dead and the woman suspected of murdering her was a woman he brought into his family lives. In a way Ralph did not mine holding his wife they had not been this intimate since they made love.

RAY WALK UP to Deidra and tap her on the shoulder. "He has a strong alibi he was home with his mother and sister besides the medical examiner found strings of hair and skin under the victim nails that don't match," Ray said. "I don't think Chavez had anything to do with this I am interested in Kim Jenkins. "Yes it is strange how she just up and disappear like that hers children and all," Ray said. "I don't know if Chavez crying about the lost of his girl or who she was laying with. "Chief we just got a call we got two more infant dead bodies that were found in the river,' Smutty the dispatcher said. Deidra hoped that this would be the end path to Kim road of carnage. Who was this women Dee thought. No one had ever heard of Kim Jenkins, no relatives, even in this small town it seem to be odd. "All cars on the lookout for Kim Jenkins last seen driving a green ford station wagon, presume dangerous," said Dee. "I going to get in touch with the residing towns near us to see if they heard of her," said Ray. "Yes, you do that, I believe we have psycho path on our hand, "said Deidra. She went towards her jeep and prepare herself see some dead babies.

After viewing, the dead little children had made Deidra Coats sick to her stomach. How could a person drown her own kids 'What kind of mercy killing if any to kill your own babies Deidra wondered? The static on her CB broke the silence in her jeep. 'Come in Ray", said Dee. "Chief we got a make on the suspect Kim Jenkins", said Ray. "Go head, "said Dee. "It seems our little Kim Jenkins is an escapee from mental institute name Little Honey's institute for young woman, "said Ray. Dee though she had a fool on the loose but not literally. "Did the ward know Jenkins is on a killing spree and theorizing my town?" Dee asked. "Yes the ward said as long she is taking her medicine she is fine w without it she is delusional and homicidal," said Ray. "When did she escape""Dee asked. "The ward says the patient Kim Bolan escape a year ago," said Ray. "Hummed so that means this fool had not had her medicine for at least a year," Deidra thought.

Deidra thinking was correct there was a fool on the loose in William Town and it would be up to her to stop her.

BISHOP CLARK WAS good at performing at funerals. You would have thought he was trying to raise the dead with his antics. He was good at falling out on the floor as if the bereavement had taken a toll on his heart. He even has been known to do a back flip a time or two. At Sal Stokes funeral he did a cartwheel for the finally of his performance. He would always start his sermon with a The Lord is good speech "Oh yes he sure is Amen and Amen again." He would say. However, at Margret's funeral he seemed to grieve sincerely. As he stood, up and looked down the isle at the grieving parents, Liz and Ralph, who was doing there best to hold their selves together. Bishop Clark started his text on thou halt not kill. "Children of William Town, the devil stays busy," preached Bishop Clark. The crowd let him know that he had an audience with their share of Amen's. "Children, the bible say he go throughout too and fro, to see what he can devoured, like this innocent child Margret," preached Bishop Clark. Liz and Ralph barely held their own. The whole time Liz was thinking how fragile life is. Ralph was thinking how he could have let someone like Kim into his family. Ralph was also thinking that he had to come clean about Kim with Liz. He figure if Liz really love him enough, she would not let twenty years go down the drain. Then Ralph also thought about the act that Kim committed to his family was unforgivable. An act the would never have taken place if had not been responsible for Kim being in William Town. Liz was so weak from grieving only Ralph seem to be the one with a grip on what was happing to his family. They had just got back from viewing Margret and she was surprise she had the strength to still be up and stirring around. Liz still had love in her heart for people, especially for her husband. There was just one thing she could not get off her mind. The day the job called Ralph for an emergency meeting. She could not get out of her head what Ralph had said to her; Liz went to lie down in her bedroom and Ralph words hit her all over again. What did he meant when he said it was probably his fault the reason why Annabelle and the whole town was sick. Something had told her to let this notion rest. However, she persisted. It had been a long day, they had just got through viewing the dead body of their firstborn and Ralph seemingly to come to grips of his family lost as the leader of his family. "Ralph let's come to bed baby", said Liz. "I am in a moment "said Ralph.

BILL WILSON, A short potbelly man, whose family owned Little Honey Mental Institute for young women, made it his job to run everything as he saw fit. The last thing he wanted was bad press. When he walks through a doorway, he tried to slam the frame each time he went through it. He rather has his employer's fear of being terminate than their loyalty to him. Yelling in a loud pitch was his way of getting his point across.

"Patrick Brian comes in my office now!" shouted Bill as if the intercom was broken. Patrick had been on the force for twenty years long enough to know a butt chewing and he would be the only person in the room with mayonnaise. He slowed down almost to a complete stop. "Here is this fool waving his hands at me dear Lord please let me keep my cool "thought Patrick.

"Come on in Brain", said Bill. He did not let on how Patrick size intimidated him. Patrick stood at 6ft.9in. In addition, was about 52in. wide in the chest Patrick easily dwarf Bill short little frame. "Brain come in here sit down ,we have a policy on negligence and laziness and quitters, I know you know the policy, I know you are not a lazy guy, so tell me Brian are you a quitter,?",asked Bill. Patrick mind went back to his days growing up as a child in Williams Town. This was his way of focusing on an object or place that made him calm, collective, and able to keep his head. Patrick had almost blocked out Bill interrogational question out of his head. Patrick had learned this technique in his martial arts training and had kept his head in many situations. I t was not his fault if little Honey 'Mental Ill Institute for Young Women did not want to invest in real security. Because in his mind that is the only way the escape happens. "Look you are my head of security, my eyes and ears, do you hear me Brian!" Bill shouted. "Yes sir!" Patrick shouted back. "The next time this happens we will be shut down for sure," said Bill. Bill went back to the intercom in his office. "Dr. Williams we need you in this office now!"Bill shouted. He looked at Patrick and deiced that he could not fire him because prior to this incident, he was a good guard and he needed him. "Go and tighten up your men Brian," said Bill.

D R. LILLIAN WILLIAMS was tiding up her desk when she heard her name on the intercom. "Now which one of Kohlberg's steps are we working with today?" Lillian wondered to herself. Lillian definitely was not going to be the fall guy for the Kim Bowen crisis. Even though she was the client therapist, she gave her synopsis on the client. Her evaluation stood on record it was Bill Wilson who did not want to inform the public of the escape. It did not take long for her to reach Bill Wilson office and get into a battle of the minds. Whatever excuse he had for her, she had an answer for him. "Lillian we are going to have answered some press about our little mishap;"Bill said. "Bill, first of all we did not have a mishap or anything else you knew the possibility of an escape and how dangerous the subject was it was your board of directors who decided to use cheap labor," said Lillian. She knew it was sheer incompetent on how her client escape and Bill Wilson nearby cover up by not informing the authorities in the neighborhoods. "Lillian all you got to do is saying we tried our best to inform the public of the escapee and we did not know the violent behavior your client poses," said Bill. "I will not," Lillian shouted. "Look Lillian play ball with us and we can get through this," said Bill. "We, look we did not have a part of this; I can only warn you of her potential without her meds. Lillian turned around and walks back into the hallway. All of her many years at Berkley had not prepare her to work for such of a second rate facility, It was the bumbling security that set steps for Kim's escape in the first place. It was then when Lillian thought of the turmoil Kim's mind was going through without her medicine. "She must be going through hell', thought Lillian.

KIM LAID FLAT on the broom closet floor with her head press to the floor as if she heard voices from it. Her plan was to meet Ralph in his office earlier the next morning. Kim felt like Ralph took full advantage of her body and her mind knowingly how she felt about him how she looked up to him. Now it was his time to pay. With that thought, she rose up and began to scrape the blade of the knife against the concrete border of the floor sharpening the blade against it. Each lie that Ralph had told her cut just like the knife she held in her hand. He had hurt her deeply in a way no man ever had. "Please don't tell me you are getting sentimental over this loser", said Larry. He had made his way back to torment Kim. "You're just weak, you thinking about hesitating aren't you bitch," screeched Larry. "Shut the Hell up Larry!" shouted Kim. Kim threw her knife at the beast as his feathers went up in the air knocking him sideways. Larry stood up back on his feet again "Um laugh that was close bitch but not close enough,"Larry laughed. He laughed aloud in a high pitch screech. All Kim could do was to beg him to stop in which that was what Larry wanted to hear her do was to beg him to stop. "Now let's try to stay focus bitch, why are we here on the floor in the first place?" Larry reminded her slyly. Kim grab her knife again and started sharpen her knife again. This time she was going to get her revenge because Ralph stood for every man that every hurt her. Kim thought of every lie ever told to her from the first time she lost her virginity ,the result of rape from Uncle Lawrence to Jim Forbes the security guard at Little Honey Academy for women and young girls, who had promise her to let her escape. All had lied and all had died. Now it was Ralph time to pay.

Liz lay down beside Ralph. She could feel the thickness in the air in the room. Something told her to lie down and go to sleep but she could not let what was on her mind rest. 'Ralph, Ralph, "Liz call. Ralph heard Liz although he laid there if he was sleep pretending not to hear. 'Ralph wake up baby I need to talk to you,' Liz said persistently. 'Yeah what's wrong?" Ralph asked. "What did you mean this was probably your fault?" Liz asked. 'Baby what in the hell you are talking about?" Ralph asked. "I am talking about the day of the outbreak when we nearly. Annabelle, you said it, what did you mean it was probably your fault?" Liz asked again. At the time when Ralph said that he thought because of his involvement with Kim was his fault that he was about to lose his little girl. He could not possible let Liz know what he meant. "Ralph why is it so hard to admit what you said?" Liz asked again. Ralph was tired of deceiving Liz but was afraid of the repercussion of telling the truth. "Liz I had an affair with a coworker at my job", Ralph blurted out. The news hit Liz like a ton of bricks. It hurt her so bad it felt like someone had kicked her in the stomach. "No this nigger didn't say what I thought he said" thought Liz. She got up and went into the bathroom. Ralph went after her "Baby please baby please it did not mean nothing" said Ralph. Liz was recovering from what Ralph confesses to her. 'Baby I did not know the girl was a stalker I "Ralph said. 'Yes you didn't know then come and lay with me like you done nothing out, out Ralph now!" Liz shouted. Angrily Liz slammed and locked the bedroom door locking Ralph out of the bedroom.

Of all the contemplating Kim had done she never contemplating Ralph kick out from his own house and coming to his own office this time of the night.

Kim heard the key chain jingle and saw the doorknob turn. She hurried on to her feet not knowing what to expect.

RALPH HAD STORMED out of the house. Not knowing what kind of replica damages he had done to his relationship. All because of a tramp, he barely even knew. I guess he was flattered when she smiled at him, it surly was not because of her past job experience that he had hired her for nor her education, no it was her bodily dimension why he had hired her. However whatever his reason he was out the door in the cold out of his own house. The only thing Ralph could focus on was his fifth of Red Bourbon he kept in his desk draw at his office. When Ralph arrived at the plant, he was surprise not to see any security at the gate; Bud Foremen usually greeted him at the gate, the guard of twenty years. Ralph thought for a minute Liz would have understood his momentary weakness. However, I guess like all other women before her time the scorn of a woman is of a great deal. The plant seem like a different place during the day than at night, the walls at night looked like giant shadows waiting to swallow you whole. Ralph had it so that he could come and go at the plant anytime he saw fit. Because his job description requires him to be, there at all times of the night folks were used to seeing him in here. People like Bud Foreman, who made it their business to know your whereabouts.

Tonight it was very odd not seeing him running up to your

car, flashing his flashlight all in your face, Ralph thought he took his job way too serious. Ralph had already decided to go home and tries to make up to Liz but he decided it would be in his best interest if she cools down.

Some times people try to work through their personal griefs and guilt. He thought he would give Liz a call and let her know that he was alrightas soon he got in his office. The phone rang and rang as if no one was there. Ralph thought that maybe this time he went to far. This time maybe it might have been much to much for Liz to take. The death of her daughter and the death of their marriage was perhaps too much to bear. Now all of this was aching Ralph head. Had it not have been for all this Ralph would have heard Kim and her knife creeping upon his body and neck. Instead, Ralph distinctly reared back like a wild mare stallion trying to bulk off his rider. However, it was a little to late of loosing Kim's vice like grip. Ralph hoped to rammed the wall with Kim's body andshe would fall loose to the groud. Ralph started to realize that his life was in jeopardy because his breathing was starting to get short. It seemed like whenever his throat was beginning to give the harder Kim squeeze. She had every intentional to kill Ralph.

Ralph was pretty damn close to passing out when the door swung open with the force of someone beautiful to Ralph eyes. Ralph wonder where Liz was at and why she did not answered her phone when he called her. He did not know that she was on her way over to his office to make up. Instead, Liz helped Ralph to kick and beat Kim ass. They took turns kicking Kim all over her body. Finally, at last Ralph stopped the attack and called the sheriff dept. Sheriff Deidra Coates was the first of her officers to pu the cuffs on Kim. "Your done, "marked Deidra.

The town of William Town seem to get back to normal with

the arrest of Kim Jenkins. Bishop Clark was still falling out and doing back fllips while looking at the women folks throughout the corner of his eyes. Maggie has started to fight crime in her very own way since she has developed a better clairvoyant gift. Ralph and Liz have learned how to appreciate each other better. Sheriff Deidra Coates became the law in William Town. The Federal prosecute has lunch a special investigation on Little Honey's Academy for Girs. However, Kim is institutionalizing again. She has calm down now with the help of her meds and the help of her straight jacket. The more she tugged and struggle the more the jacket seem to hug her. All Kim could do was count the buttons on her patted wall of her eight by nine ft. cell. Her life sentence was living in this confine cell away from society where she would do no harm ever again. Yes, but she did had the doctor's fooled before? All it takes is a pretty smile and grin and all of your guard would fall down. Then the next thing that you will feel is the sharp blade of her butcher knife. Then last fragments of air leaving your body as you gurgle for help.

About the Author

CJ MOORE GREW up in the rural town of Blount's Creek, North Carolina. He attended Fayetteville State University in Fayetteville, North Carolina, and Western International University in Phoenix, Arizona. Now a bilateral above-the-knee amputee, Cj is learning to walk again. This is his debut novel.